THE HILLS OF HOME

Melanie's new employer is Linda Fletcher-Grant, who is rarely out of the gossip columns. Linda mistrusts the press, so Melanie doesn't mention that her fiancé, Paul, is a journalist. Melanie needs time to think about her shaky engagement and is immediately attracted to Conrad, Linda's estate manager. Then Paul turns up, determined to cause trouble. But is there any point in Melanie staying when Conrad is engaged to marry Helen and is already making plans for travelling home to Vermont?

PATRICIA McAUGHEY

THE HILLS OF HOME

Complete and Unabridged

LINFORD
Leicester

First published in Great Britain in 1991 by
Robert Hale Limited
London

First Linford Edition
published 2001
by arrangement with
Robert Hale Limited
London

British Library CIP Data

McAughey, Patricia
    The hills of home.—Large print ed.—
Linford romance library
    1. Love stories
    2. Large type books
    I. Title
    823.9'14 [F]

    ISBN 0–7089–4573–2

Published by
F. A. Thorpe (Publishing)
Anstey, Leicestershire

Set by Words & Graphics Ltd.
Anstey, Leicestershire
Printed and bound in Great Britain by
T. J. International Ltd., Padstow, Cornwall

This book is printed on acid-free paper

She was late. Melanie drove the car to a halt outside the imposing entrance to Headmoor Hall and peered nervously through the rain-splashed windscreen.

She switched off the engine and sighed, rubbing at the mud stain on her cream dress. Oh heavens, she had made it worse! Why had she bothered to stop at that cafe on the moor road? She might have known from its appearance that it would serve a mediocre cup of coffee. Dashing back to the car, she had been caught in a heavy downpour and, in addition to that, she had still managed to trip in a pot-hole in the car-park despite the waitress's cheerful warning.

She had splattered her dress and wrenched her ankle, the three-inch heels on her new cream interview shoes hardly helping. Oh well, she was so late

minutes would
... that a few ...nd she needed a
... o differ...pose herself. She
... ...ent to ...handbag to check the
reached for ...re. She extracted the
letter was... of paper and read it again.
single she...
It was written on pale pink writing-paper, hardly suitable for a business letter, and informally signed 'Linda Shelley'. The signature was enormous and extravagantly looped, and somehow, despite the frivolity of the notepaper or maybe because of it, she thought she would like Linda Shelley.

She replaced it in her bag, glancing once more towards the house. It was bucketing down and she had no umbrella, not even a jacket, so she would simply have to dash the few yards to the entrance. It looked very grand and she hesitated. Should she use the front door or would it be more appropriate to find a door round the back? The tradesmen's entrance! Why on earth should she, she wasn't a tradesman, was she? Irritated at herself

1

She was late. Melanie drew the car to a halt outside the imposing entrance to Headmoor Hall and peered nervously through the rain-splashed windscreen.

She switched off the engine and sighed, rubbing at the mud stain on her cream dress. Oh heavens, she had made it worse! Why had she bothered to stop at that cafe on the moor road? She might have known from its appearance that it would serve a mediocre cup of coffee. Dashing back to the car, she had been caught in a heavy downpour and, in addition to that, she had still managed to trip in a pot-hole in the car-park despite the waitress's cheerful warning.

She had splattered her dress and wrenched her ankle, the three-inch heels on her new cream interview shoes hardly helping. Oh well, she was so late already that a few more minutes would make no difference and she needed a moment to compose herself. She reached for her handbag to check the letter was there. She extracted the single sheet of paper and read it again. It was written on pale pink writing-paper, hardly suitable for a business letter, and informally signed 'Linda Shelley'. The signature was enormous and extravagantly looped, and some-how, despite the frivolity of the notepaper or maybe because of it, she thought she would like Linda Shelley.

She replaced it in her bag, glancing once more towards the house. It was bucketing down and she had no umbrella, not even a jacket, so she would simply have to dash the few yards to the entrance. It looked very grand and she hesitated. Should she use the front door or would it be more appropriate to find a door round the back? The tradesmen's entrance! Why on earth should she, she wasn't a tradesman, was she? Irritated at herself for wasting yet more time, she stepped out into the sheet of rain and slammed the car door shut, walking as briskly as her heels would allow towards the porch. Head bent, she did not notice the bulky shape before her until it was too late and she was held in its firm grip.

She disentangled herself with a low grumble. 'I didn't see you,' she muttered by way of a grudging apology. 'The rain's so . . . I was trying to . . . ' her words tailed off as the man gave a deep chuckle that she found immensely irritating.

'Miss Lawrence, I presume?' he said, amusement clearly etched in his voice. 'You're late.'

'I know,' Melanie said coolly, not volunteering that she had got lost once she had left the moor road. The rain was lashing against her face, the wind whipping up wispy strands of hair. It was all right for him for he was wearing a roomy jacket, the hood pulled up partially obscuring his face.

'We'd better not tramp mud through the hall,' he said. 'Come this way instead.' He set off quickly, too quickly, causing her to clatter along after him trying to keep up with his long strides. Where was he taking her? The rain was by now torrential, bouncing off the path as they followed it towards the side of the house. As they turned the corner, a gust of wind took her breath away and above her, low-slung branches dislodged a spray of water.

'Nearly there,' he shouted back over the noise of the wind. 'It's a bit muddy just here.'

'Thank you *very* much for telling me,' Melanie said, her sarcasm lost in the storm. She retrieved her shoe and slipped her wet foot back into it before following him into the calm of a large conservatory. She scarcely had time to admire the bright array of pot plants and hanging baskets before he was off again, discarding his coat casually on a hook in the narrow passage.

He ran a hand through dark, curly

hair before turning to smile at her. 'Conrad Bailes,' he said, extending his hand. 'Welcome to Headmoor! Pity it's raining, it's blocked out the view over the fells.'

She was past caring about views. She held out her own hand politely. His grip was firm, warm, his eyes a most unusual blue, his features neatly and attractively chiselled into a pleasant, if not totally handsome face. Beyond him, she caught sight of her reflection in a mirror. 'Oh heavens, look at me,' she wailed. 'I look terrible.'

'You do look a bit of a mess,' he agreed with a disarming grin. 'I've never seen anyone look quite so drenched and sorry for herself.'

Well, really, there was no need for him to be quite so honest. Her glare was wasted on him as he shot off into a kitchen where a grey-haired woman was clearing up a scrubbed central table. 'There you are at last,' she said, beaming a smile of welcome. 'Conrad, did you have to bring her all the way round? Look at her, she's soaked.' She shook her head sadly. 'It'd never occur to him to take an umbrella round for you.' Her tone clearly implied 'men!'

'You'd never keep one up in that wind,' Conrad argued, amiably enough. 'This is Miss Lawrence, Jean.' He turned to Melanie. 'And this is Jean Cookson. She's the best cook in the whole world but we keep quiet about it. We don't want her getting ideas above her station, do we?'

'Shut up, Conrad,' Jean said, unable to disguise her pleased smile. Her eyes were kind under a pair of heavy-rimmed spectacles. She took in Melanie's bedraggled appearance once more and sighed. 'Would you like to freshen up, dear, before you go in? Conrad will show you where the cloakroom is.'

'Thank you.' Melanie was suddenly aware of the man towering beside her. He was powerfully built, his shoulders broad under the blue of his sweater. It matched his eyes rather well but he did not look the sort of man who had deliberately gone for the effect it produced. He had a tanned, open-air face with a faint trace of shadow on his chin and his hair, very dark brown, was just a fraction longer than current fashion decreed.

Once in the cloakroom, Melanie eyed herself with increasing dismay. Was this really the same girl who had set off from home this morning? Crept off, in fact, before her mother could see her and start asking awkward questions. She had selected the cream dress with such care, an elegant, classical shirt-waister, and now look at it. And look at her hair! So much for the neat bob she had painstakingly blown into shape. Her make-up was by now non-existent, her cheeks flushed and damp, her eyes bright. Quickly, she towelled her hair dry then tipped the contents of her bag out and set to work. She was not surprised that her chestnut-gold hair had refused to remain in the confines of the bob. Giving up, she brushed it into its usual looser style, applied shadow and mascara and fresh lipstick, then splashed herself liberally, if a little extravagantly, with the perfume Paul had given her for Christmas.

There! Her light-brown, gold-flecked eyes stared back mournfully. How unprepared she had turned out to be for this interview. What she ought to have done, what anyone with an ounce of sense would have done, was to have brought a change of clothes and a spare pair of stockings just in case something like this should happen. She should never have trusted the weather forecast even if this side of the Pennines was supposed to be drier than the west.

But then she was a little naïve when it came to interviews and, because she had wanted to keep this one a secret, she had been unable to discuss it with anyone, least of all to ask for advice. Her last interview, her only one come to that, had been with her present employers when she was just seventeen and fresh out of secretarial college.

Seven years ago and Mr Johnson had put her at ease at once in that special, fatherly way of his. The guilty feeling surfaced once more. How could she think of walking out just when the company was going through a difficult patch. She hoped Mr Johnson would understand that her leaving was nothing to do with that.

She was worrying about nothing, she told herself firmly, clicking the clasp on her bag, as the chances of getting this job were now so remote. Who would want to employ a girl who arrived late with her dress smudged and stockings laddered? She examined the ladder worriedly. It was only a little one, hardly noticeable, and surely preferable to arriving for an interview bare-legged.

Conrad was waiting as she emerged and she was aware at once of the flicker of admiration in his eyes as he smiled reassuringly. 'Don't look so worried,' he said. 'She won't bite. She's not half so bad as her reputation suggests.'

Puzzled by the remark, she neverthe-less gave him a grateful smile and followed him through a gracious hall, stopping in front of a dark, panelled door.

Conrad tapped on it and opened it on hearing a woman's voice. He announced her, then whispered, 'Good luck,' as she stepped past him into the room.

A blue-green sea of carpet led towards the woman draped on one of the enormous white leather sofas. The room was light and airy with an ornate ceiling and magnificient chandelier. Palest green curtains framed two tall, narrow windows overlooking the garden.

Melanie advanced warily over the deep pile, noticing as she neared the slim figure that she was considerably older than she had at first thought, cleverly understated make-up not quite able to disguise the signs of late middle-age.

Her ash-blonde hair had no trouble

remaining in its deceptively simple long bob and she was wearing pale green that matched her eyes, but this time Melanie guessed she would be all too aware of the startling effect. Bare feet with red-tipped nails peeped out from the hem of silk lounging-pyjamas. Melanie had expected a desk, a suit, much more formality, although maybe the pink writing-paper ought to have given her a clue.

'You're late, Miss Lawrence.' It was not a rebuke and the smile was wide and welcoming. 'We're not easy to find. I'm afraid I'm hopeless at giving directions. I expect you took the wrong turning just before the village. Everyone does.' The smile stayed. 'My late husband's colleagues used to get themselves hopelessly lost on the moors. Winters here can be quite dreadful. We once rescued a friend just in the nick of time before a blizzard buried him forever.'

She paused and motioned towards the opposite sofa. 'Do sit down. You

11

look quite chilled. Have you had a truly dreadful journey?' Another torrent of words began to spill out as Melanie struggled to think of something intelligent to say. 'Would you like to step out of that damp dress, my dear? I can find you something to wear in the meantime.'

'No, no thank you. I'm fine,' Melanie said, not wanting to cause any more fuss. She obligingly perched on the sofa near the fire, adjusting a mountain of lacy cushions as she did so.

'So you are Melanie Lawrence.' Out of nowhere, Melanie's letter of application had appeared. 'Most impressive qualifications. Your personal reference was outstanding.' A small smile hovered. 'I quite understand you not wishing to supply an employer's reference yet. Sometimes it pays to be discreet. And I think I can trust you.' The smile vanished and the green eyes regarded her calmly. 'That's all I really require of the people in my employ. Trust. I once employed a junior maid who let us down badly. She was dishonest, a thief, and I was forced to sack her and, out of spite, she blabbed this ridiculous story to the papers. All-night parties, drunken orgies. I was livid.'

'Oh . . . ' Melanie bit her lip. Something was stirring in her memory. There was something vaguely familiar about the face opposite. But what?

'You haven't recognized me, have you?' The laugh was genuine, head thrown back in delight. 'What a relief! I'm Linda Fletcher-Grant, my dear, and I do apologize for the ridiculous subterfuge. Linda Shelley indeed!' The underlying laughter disappeared as she leaned forward intently. 'There was a reason for it,' she said. 'I thought it unwise to use my real name. I just didn't want people applying for the wrong reasons.'

Astounded at the turn the conversation had taken, Melanie murmured that she quite understood.

'Do you?' The tone was amused. 'I

wonder? It all happened before your time, my dear. Your father will be au fait with it, I expect. As for the press, the least said about them the better. They've got ridiculously long memories. I'm forever branded as a scarlet woman. Do you see me as one?'

'Good heavens, no,' Melanie said at once. 'People of my generation don't worry about things like that. We wouldn't bat an eyelid these days.' She blushed as she realized that was a less than flattering statement to the still attractive woman before her.

To her relief, Linda laughed; an open, honest laugh. 'Good for you,' she said. 'How refreshing! It's not quite true, of course; I'm afraid these things do still matter. People even today can be very narrow-minded. As far as Philip and I were concerned, it was always a non-story but ... oh, it's all too boring.' Deliberately she returned her attention to Melanie's letter. 'Now, let's see, where were we?' She scanned the page swiftly. 'The only reservation I

14

have is this . . . ' She gazed solidly at Melanie. 'Why do you want to shut yourself away up here? There's nothing except sheep and moors and the occasional sleepy village. Nothing happens. The nearest town is twenty miles away and even that boasts only one or two department stores. Can you, a town girl like you, possibly bear it?' Her smile, an attractive one, crept upon her once more. 'In other words, my dear, what are you trying to escape from?' She waited, smoothing a non-existent crease on her pale-green lap. Her hands were beautifully manicured, with several large diamond rings adorning them.

Melanie glanced down at her own hands, bare of rings because she had chosen to leave Paul's emerald one at home. 'I'm not trying to escape from anything,' she said quietly, knowing as she said it that it was not true. She *was* trying to escape but she wanted this job and was wary of saying anything that might put Linda off her. 'I never

15

meant to stay so long at Johnson's,' she began. That, at least, was perfectly true. 'Apart from Mr Johnson, who's a lovely man, I don't come into contact with people very much. It's all a bit boring.' She paused, her enthusiasm catching up with her. 'This job sounds really exciting. Working on a book. I should love to work on a book. And I need to get away from home,' she added thoughtfully. 'I live with my parents and it's time I became independent.'

Linda raised her eyebrows. 'It certainly is. But a new job and a new home? Is that wise? Are you quite sure? What if you hate it here? You won't get your old job back, will you, and this is only temporary, until my book's finished. Can you afford to take the chance?'

'I must,' Melanie said firmly. 'I have to. I've promised myself. And there are always openings for good secretaries,' she added with a smile, displaying more confidence than she felt. 'I'll love it here. I love the country. It'll be so relaxing.'

'It's relaxing all right,' Linda echoed, a touch drily. 'Idyllic in fact. I'd go mad if I didn't get into town at least twice a month. By town, I mean London of course. We have a mews flat there. Philip never cared much for it but it's my lifeline. I fly down. It takes no time at all.' She smiled, crossing one leg over the other, wiggling her red-tipped toes. 'Now, let's get down to the nitty-gritty, Melanie. The work will certainly be interesting as I don't know where to start. I'll need your help. I'm a complete amateur when it comes to writing. A friend of mine in publishing is very keen for me to do this and he's offered help, but I don't want a ghost-writer. I want to do it myself, so I'm sure it's *my* book. It can't be that difficult, surely? It will simply be a matter of getting some sort of plan worked out.' Her smile was infectious. 'I'm so looking forward to it. What do you think? Will you be able to help me?'

'I'll love it,' Melanie said eagerly. 'I love organizing my own work-schedules. Mr Johnson has always left that side of things to me and things have run smoothly enough.'

'That's settled then. The job's yours if you still want it,' Linda said abruptly. 'Have you a boyfriend, Melanie?'

Taken aback by the sudden question, Melanie was saved an immediate reply by the arrival of Jean with a tea-tray. Linda introduced Melanie as her new PA and Jean's approval was evident from her broad smile as she left them alone once more. Linda began to pour tea into pretty china cups.

'I always take quick decisions,' she said. 'Although not always the right ones,' she added ruefully. 'I've only interviewed one other girl for this and she was so pop-eyed when she realized who I was that she couldn't speak. This so-called fame amazes me.' She handed Melanie a cup and looked at her thoughtfully. 'It's not as if I've ever done anything, is it, except marry

18

Philip. He was a brilliant man with a quite extraordinary brain. He was much in demand as an after-dinner speaker, although often I suspected people were curious as to what I was really like . . . ' She paused. 'I mustn't bore you. I do tend to go on a bit about him. You see, I . . . ' She bit her lip, struggling a little with her expression. 'Are you going to take the job? I'll match your present salary, of course, and you'll have free accommodation and your weekends will be free too. How does that sound?' She nodded with satisfaction at Melanie's pleased smile. 'Good. Then that's settled. I hope you'll like your room. It's a small suite, in fact, because we've acres of space here. This was to have been the perfect family home, meant for lots of children. It's far too big for me now I'm alone, but I don't want to leave. Not yet.'

Looking at her, it dawned on Melanie that precious few weeks had elapsed since Philip Fletcher-Grant's sudden death. She ought to offer a word of condolence, but even as she debated what to say, Linda had moved determinedly on. 'Philip loved the country,' she continued. 'And I love it too in my own way. You don't have to wear tweeds and twin-sets, although some of our friends think you do. You should see the things they bring with them for a country weekend.' She laughed and, at last, Melanie began to relax, sitting more comfortably on the sofa, her toes warm from the proximity of the log fire.

'Jean's a real gem,' Linda said, the abrupt change of subject taking Melanie by surprise. 'I don't know what I would have done without her after Philip died. Conrad, too, was a wonderful help. He's my estate manager and a great organizer. He kept the press at bay when the news broke. Personally, I believe they were quite delighted at the way things turned out. Some sort of ironic revenge. Wouldn't you have thought they would have had the decency to . . . I despise journalists.' Her eyes filled with tears and she wiped them away with a lace handkerchief, the gesture managing to be simultaneously natural and theatrical. 'Philip had a heart problem which he preferred not to discuss and he was no longer young, so, in some ways, it was no surprise. It was just the timing.' She replaced her cup on the tray. 'That's why I have to write the book. My story. It's time I set the record straight. People have always been so unsympathetic to me and it hurts, and I owe it to Philip to tell the truth because so many people thought badly of him too and he was the most wonderful man. Believe me, Melanie, the whole thing was blown up out of all proportion.'

Melanie smiled gently. She knew little enough about this. Hadn't there been some indiscreet love-affair many years ago? Philip Fletcher-Grant had been a highly-respected businessman as well as a reluctant television personality, the last person to get involved in a thing like that. Why all the fuss? It happened every day surely. If anyone had got this thing out of proportion, it seemed to be Linda, who was treating the press as if they had pursued some sort of vendetta against her. At the moment, however, it seemed wise to agree with her, hence the gentle smile. Now was not the moment to argue about the respective merits of journalists. Paul was a journalist, and a very good one.

'Now you were just about to tell me about this boyfriend of yours,' Linda said disconcertingly, as if reading her mind. 'And don't tell me you haven't one. You're far too pretty not to have a boyfriend.'

'I . . . do have a boyfriend,' Melanie began hesitantly, her rehearsed words on this subject deserting her. Getting this job would be the first step to independence and she wanted the job desperately. She was loath to say anything that might put Linda off her, even at this stage. What would Linda say if she knew that she was in the throes of marriage plans? The pressure on her to go through with it was immense and it would take tremendous courage to put the brakes on it. 'I'm engaged,' she said with a sigh. 'Paul wants to marry me and I thought at first that I wanted that too. Our families are great friends and they almost willed it on us. I've known him since I was a little girl and, as you can imagine, everyone's so thrilled. It's going to be so difficult.' She smiled with an effort, sensing the sympathy in the other woman's eyes. 'What do I do? Paul's father has bought us a little terraced house to start off in and I feel so ungrateful. Mother says it's just pre-wedding nerves but I . . . feel trapped. I have to get away for a while, to have time to think.' She took a deep breath and raised her head in a sudden spirited show of confidence. 'You needn't worry about the job, Mrs Fletcher-Grant, I'll put everything I have into that; and if, by the end of our contract, I find I can't bear life without Paul, I'll marry him.'

'I thought as much,' Linda said

triumphantly. 'I knew there was a problem with your love-life and I'm not usually wrong. So, that's what you're running away from, my dear, and you expect me to aid and abet you. What does this Paul of yours think about it all?'

'He doesn't know yet,' Melanie told her miserably. 'I'm dreading telling him. He's going to be so upset. And I can't imagine what my mother will say. She's booked the reception and bought her outfit. She'll be furious. The whole thing will ruin her socially.'

Linda laughed and apologized for doing so. 'Are you really twenty-four, Melanie? You seem younger. You allow people to manipulate you.' She paused and peered intently at her finger-nails. 'You must tell this young man of yours at once and, if he loves you, he'll understand. He'll be hurt no doubt, but he'll understand and give you the time you need. As for your mother and her feelings, well really . . . if all she's concerned about is her outfit and what people will say, then it's too bad.' Her eyes twinkled. 'The job's still yours despite your confession. I can see I might well be called upon to be an agony aunt. Do feel free to unburden yourself on me. I feel I might rather enjoy that.'

'Thank you,' Melanie murmured in relief. 'I won't let you down, Mrs Fletcher-Grant.'

'No, I'm sure you won't,' Linda said, smiling in her friendly fashion. 'And, for goodness' sake, do please call me Linda. I can't bear formality.'

Melanie agreed a little shyly. She would have preferred to keep their relationship on a more business-like footing, but who was she to argue with her prospective boss? Once again, she should have realized from the very start, from the pink writing-paper, that this job would be much different from Johnson's and its rather staid image.

'Come upstairs and I'll show you your room,' Linda said, rising gracefully. She was surprisingly tiny, several inches shorter than Melanie's own not very impressive five-foot-four.

They climbed a curving staircase, past beautiful pieces of antique furniture. Wherever possible, bowls of spring flowers in pretty containers lightened what was predominantly a dark stair-well. Large gilt-framed oil-paintings added to the grandeur. It was museum-like but also a home, down to the aroma of something cooking.

'Your rooms are at the back of the house overlooking the river,' Linda said, opening a door and letting Melanie step by. She was delighted with her first glimpse of the small sitting-room. Yellow and white, it managed to be sunny despite the grey day. Off to one side, there was a feminine bedroom and a stark black and white bathroom softened by thoughtful posies of flowers and colourful accessories.

'Like it?' The question was unnecessary and Linda's smile was that of a child showing off its favourite toy. 'There's even a balcony,' she said in delight. 'Come and see.'

French windows opened out onto the balcony and they stood quietly, side by side, admiring the sweeping views of the terraced rear gardens. The mist had lifted, the rain had stopped, and a watery sun was peeping hesitantly through a veil of clouds. There was even a rainbow disappearing amongst the bank of trees that almost hid the river from sight.

Linda waved her hand vaguely. 'We own all this as well as quite a bit more all over the county. Philip's family goes back a long way. For generations.' She sighed, leaning against the balustrade, tracing her hand along its rough surface. 'It's such a pity that, after all this time, the line's finally stopped. It was a great sadness to him. Eleanor, his first wife, was unable to have children either.'

Melanie held her breath, not daring to disturb the poignancy of the moment with trivial chat. Fortunately, she was beginning to realize that Linda's unhappy moments were short-lived, and sure enough her next words were spoken in a much lighter vein, as she pointed out the far-flung corners of the vast estate. 'Most of the cottages are ours,' she said. 'Conrad's in overall charge and he's my contact with our tenants. Oh, talk of the devil, there he is.'

She had seen him too as he strode across the lawns towards the house, his movements athletic and easy, thoroughly at home in his surroundings.

'Attractive, isn't he?' Linda murmured, glancing at her slyly. 'What do you make of him?'

'He seems a very nice man,' Melanie said lamely, not quite sure what to say and suddenly wishing to avoid eye-contact with Linda. Her heart had given an unexpected hiccup at the sight of him. What on earth was the matter with her today? She'd only just met the man for heaven's sake.

'He is nice,' Linda agreed, as they stepped back into the room. 'Poor dear.

He's just been through this traumatic experience with Helen. I've told him he mustn't blame himself but it's not easy when you love someone and you think you're to blame for hurting them.' She stopped, catching sight of Melanie's puzzled expression. 'I'm sorry, I shouldn't have mentioned it. He'll tell you about it in his own time. I'm going to miss him so much when he goes. If he goes,' she added with a small smile that did not quite reach her eyes. 'Come on, I'm getting morbid. Let's go back down and I'll show you the office. It's just been redecorated. It used to be Philip's domain and I wanted something a little more feminine.'

Bemused, Melanie followed her. Who was Helen? Whoever she was, she was important to Conrad and somehow that irked her. She had assumed him to be unmarried, although she had no basis for that assumption. Wishful thinking maybe!

She pulled her thoughts together

sharply. Now that was absurd with Paul waiting at home, still expecting her to be marrying him later in the summer. Paul was generally regarded as a good catch. His father had built up a thriving business and, although Paul had not followed him into that, he had inherited his father's ambition. He was going to make a name for himself in journalism, and moving someday from the provincial paper he at present worked on was already on his mind. He was ambitious to the point of frenzy and it worried Melanie. Would he ever be satisfied with his lot? The tiny terraced house was just a beginning. There would be better things to come and, knowing Paul, Melanie believed that to be true. So, what was wrong with her? Why all these silly doubts? He loved her. Hadn't he told her that? And she loved him. Didn't she? How did you know these things?

★　★　★

'I assume you're used to modern office-equipment.' Linda's cool voice interrupted her disturbed thoughts. 'I don't know a thing about it and I'm very gullible to salesmen's patter. He had the most attractive moustache and it quite put me off my stride.' She giggled and managed to carry it off. In some women of her age a giggle would have been repellent. 'I bought everything,' she continued proudly. 'The lot. He said the word processor was an absolute must in this day and age. I only hope you know what to do with it, Melanie, because I haven't a clue. He did give me a demonstration but it quite bewildered me.'

'I already operate one,' Melanie said calmly, looking round the office. It was about the size of hers and Mr Johnson's combined, with a distracting view of the fells from two large windows elaborately curtained in plum-coloured velvet. A large decorative desk with two equally decorative telephones occupied one corner whilst the word processor and other pieces of expensive equipment were on more functional desks. The colour scheme was a most un-office-like pale pink with a deeper pink carpet, and flowers in toning colours were on every available surface.

Linda followed her gaze. 'Most offices are so drab,' she said, a little defensively. 'Why should they be? I love pink. That's why I use it for my correspondence, personal or not. It's so unexpected. It amuses me.'

But instead she looked vulnerable and suddenly very much the newly widowed lady that she was. Melanie was quite convinced she had loved her late husband. How then could she explain that last incriminating photograph? It was supposed to have precipitated Philip's fatal heart attack. It had shown Linda looking up adoringly into the eyes of a much younger man. Not just any man either but Christofer-Jon, one of the brightest hairdressers on the London scene. He was Canadian-born and was fast acquiring a reputation for becoming romantically involved with an assortment of up-and-coming actresses. It was rather the in-thing to be seen being escorted by him but his association with Linda was something of a shock. Wearing a dress with a plunging neckline and looking half her age *and* dining cosily with him had been the stuff journalists dream of.

Melanie realized that mentioning that must remain strictly out of bounds. Linda might like their relationship to be informal but it was still that of employer and employee and Melanie was determined not to forget that. Quickly, she steered the conversation onto the working aspects of the room. She would enjoy working here in this calm, pretty environment. After the sombre working conditions at Johnson's, the contrast was unnerving but welcome.

After a brief tour through the other downstairs rooms, the interview was at an end. Conrad was summoned to escort her to the car whilst Linda retired to bed with a sudden headache.

Melanie waited in the hall in some embarrassment for him to appear. 'So you got the job?' he said cheerfully. 'Well done! I don't envy you. She's got a butterfly mind and trying to pin her down won't be easy.'

'I'll cope,' Melanie said thoughtfully, pushing back a heavy fold of hair and stealing a glance at him.

They walked past her car to look at the lawns spread before them, gently drying as the sun gained confidence. 'It's lovely here,' she murmured. 'I had no idea I would be working for her, for Linda Fletcher-Grant. It came as a complete surprise.'

He chuckled. 'Just like her. She likes the dark glasses and incognito bit. I think she imagines that everyone's heard of her, and that's not true. Sometimes I wonder if she doesn't go out of her way to do something outrageous to get her name back in the papers.'

'Oh that's not fair,' Melanie said hotly. 'I'm sure that's not true. She seems really upset at the fuss.'

He shrugged, gazing towards the blurry hills. 'I'm sorry, maybe you're right. They were happy enough together and I should know. I've been around for the last ten years.'

'You've worked for Linda for ten years?' She smiled up at him. She loved his voice. Dark and quiet and hypnotic. Soothing.

'But maybe not for much longer,' he said after a moment. 'I've got the chance of a job back home.'

'Home? Where's that?'

'The States.' He grinned. 'No, don't tell me, I know I've lost my American accent, but I did live there for quite a few years when I was growing up. My dad was a director of a chemical company and he helped set up the American factory.'

'Is he still there?'

'No. Mum always wanted to come back to England when they retired and they've done just that. They live in a thatched cottage in Dorset. It's what she dreamed about and they're happy there. I came back to go to university and just stayed on.'

'But you still think of America as home? That will be because you were a child then,' Melanie said thoughtfully. 'Childhood memories are always so special. I think we all have a soft spot for the place we grew up in.'

'You're right.' There was the ghost of a smile on his face. 'I've been offered this job, chance of a partnership with a friend of mine. He's opening this motel and restaurant by the lake. Lake Champlain, on the Vermont side.' For a moment he seemed lost in thought. 'It's beautiful there. I can't describe it. Space. Hills. The lake. I love hills. Without them, I feel homesick and . . . ' He stopped and she sensed his sudden embarrassment.

'I know exactly how you feel.' To ease the awkwardness for him, she created a diversion by rummaging in her bag. 'I must go,' she said brightly. 'I've got a two-hour drive ahead of me.'

'When will we be seeing you again?'

'About a month I expect. I have to give my notice in and show the new girl the ropes.' A vision of Mr Johnson's pleasant face made her uncomfortable. It would be such a shock for him when she told him she was leaving. His recent illness had forced him to rely on her even more than usual and the feeling that she was being disloyal would not go away.

She held out her hand and Conrad clasped it, smiling disturbingly right into her eyes and causing her to fumble with the door lock in sudden helpless confusion. He made no move to help, as Paul would have rushed to do, but merely watched as she inserted the key at last into the lock and stepped into the car.

'Are you going to drive in those shoes?'

'These?' She looked down at them as if she had never seen them before. 'Oh yes. I'm quite used to it. I always drive in these sort of shoes.'

'You shouldn't.' His face had clouded, his tone was serious. 'They don't give you enough control of the pedals.'

'Nonsense. I'm quite used to it,' she said crisply. Privately, she had to concede that her shoes might not be entirely suitable for driving but it was no concern of his and it irritated her that he should assume it was. One thing about Paul, he had never once remarked on her shoes, although, to be honest, she sat in the passenger seat when she was with him.

'Goodbye then,' she said, refusing to take it too seriously. 'I'll look forward to seeing you all again.'

She set off smoothly, glancing repeatedly into the mirror until the curve of the drive lost him. As he disappeared, she felt a strange loss. She drove onto the moor road, relief flooding over her. She had got the job against all odds surely. This morning she had been hopeful but not very confident, but she had done it. Her satisfied smile broke up as she contemplated what lay ahead. She would have to enlist her father's help. He alone would understand. If her instinct was right, he had never been quite so overjoyed at the prospective match as her mother. As for Paul, he would understand, wouldn't he? She was simply asking for a postponement to the wedding. She was aware how difficult it would be, with arrangements under way, but what difference would a few months make to a lifetime together? She just needed to be absolutely sure. Sometimes Paul was so gentle. She recalled the first time he had kissed her. She had been at a very low ebb upon the death of her beloved pet and Paul had just happened to be there. His comforting kiss had changed suddenly and they had looked at each other with a rare wonder. But the gentle moments were less and less. His passion quite overwhelmed her. He was trying to hurry her and when she did not want to be hurried, he accused her of being cold. Paul loved her. So he said. But even as she tried to curb the rising panic within her, she knew that he would be blazingly angry. She had been a fool to let things get so far. She should have stopped it before it even started.

She thought of Conrad. Now there was a man who would have understood her turmoil. She did not know him at all and yet oddly she felt she did. There had been a spark of excitement between them, making her want to reach out and touch him. How extraordinary! She had felt glowingly alive. Was that love at first sight?

She laughed aloud. Ridiculous, she had never believed in that. It only happened in books, didn't it? In real life, everyone knew that love grew slowly, developed as your knowledge and understanding of your partner developed, strengthened as the years passed. And yet . . .

'You do look a bit of a mess,' he had said. Not very flattering, yet at the time undeniably true. The cheek of it! Why then, did she find herself smiling at the memory?

She slowed as she came up behind a lorry struggling up the steep incline. The hills were less impressive now that she was almost on top of them. They were mere bumps, covered in coarse heather and bracken. Less impressive maybe, but still beautiful. She knew exactly what Conrad meant. Hills did that to her too. It was almost a spiritual feeling. She could never talk about things like that with Paul. He was far too practical and down-to-earth, always on the look-out for a story, and very much a town person. He would think her quite mad to consider living here in the country. She smiled. It had caught her far more than she had thought it would. The peace. The stillness. The majesty of the soaring hills. She had forgotten how lovely the countryside was, and now she was going to be a part of it, living here.

Her spirits lifted as she breasted the hill and, as if sensing her mood, the sun shook itself free of one last, stubborn cloud and dazzled her.

2

Panic took over as she neared home. Lorna Kirkbride, Paul's mother, was every bit as formidable in her way as Melanie's mother, and she would be speechless with horror. The two were forever meeting for coffee and the biggest problem on their agenda at the moment stretched to what colour the bridesmaids should wear. Lorna favoured peach but Melanie's mother had suggested lemon. Oddly, it did not occur to them to ask Melanie which she preferred. Too wrapped up in her own worries of late, Melanie saw that she had let things slide over her much too often. To be assertive now, at this late stage, would be doubly difficult.

The traffic was heavy on the outskirts of town and she was thankful for the calmer roads of the leafy suburb where she lived. Guiltily she drove past St

Mary's Church where she was to be married, even more guiltily past the end of Park Terrace where Johnson's dingy works was situated, and parked her car at last in the drive of her parents' home.

Her father would be alone and for that at least she was grateful. She needed time to compose herself after the long drive before she faced her mother. She needed to tell someone and that someone had to be Dad. With an effort, she forced a cheerfulness into her voice as she announced her arrival.

He was in the sitting-room in his favourite armchair. He had been asleep judging by his tousled appearance and sleepy eyes. His slow, familiar smile was comforting.

'Hello, love. Enjoy your day off?' He yawned hugely. 'Your mother was a bit put out at the way you sneaked off without telling her where you were off to. She doesn't like secrets.'

'I'll tell you later.' Melanie tugged at her dress. 'Look at the state of this. I got soaked.'

44

'Did you now?' He raised his eyebrows. 'It's been a nice day here,' he added with a grin. 'And you look pleased with yourself. What have you been up to?'

'I'll tell you *later*,' Melanie repeated with a smile. 'Put the kettle on, Dad, while I get changed.'

Later, comfortably settled on the old sofa, her legs tucked up beneath her, she told him. He registered little surprise, merely puffed a little more extravagantly on his pipe. 'Sounds like a good job,' he admitted. 'Though I'm not so sure about you working for that madam. You don't know the half of that story.'

'I can imagine,' Melanie said drily. 'Did the headline say something like 'Millionaire leaves wife for teenage bride'?'

He smiled. 'Not far out. You're not Paul's fiancée for nothing.' He sobered a little, remembering. 'Not that he gave up that much. He didn't give up the money. You can't help thinking that's

45

what she married him for, can you? A slip of a girl like that? Mind you, he lost his chance of a career in Parliament. We wouldn't have it, would we? People in the public eye have got to set a standard.'

'Oh, Dad, don't be so pompous.'

'You can't change the facts, love,' he said patiently. 'And the fact was he left his wife, his invalid wife at that, for a teenage floozie, some sort of actress with blonde hair and baby blue eyes.'

'She's got green eyes,' Melanie corrected him mischievously. 'So they got that wrong for a start.'

He puffed at his pipe, a glimmer of amusement in his eyes. 'All right then, what's she like?'

'I thought you'd never ask.' Melanie thought a moment. 'I liked her. She's still very attractive and a bit flamboyant I suppose. Yes, she does look like an actress.' She bit her lip and swept an awkward fold of hair off her face. 'I'm going to take the job, Dad. Nobody's going to make me change my mind about that.'

'Pity to leave Johnson's though,' he said quietly. 'You've done well there. You've worked yourself up into a good position.'

She pulled a face. 'To what? Mr Johnson's secretary. The work's dull, Dad, and you know it. You know I've not been happy there for ages. I want something different, and living and working up there will be different, won't it?'

'I don't know what your mother will say. She's got lists written already. Invitations. Food. Presents. Flowers. And what about this Paul of yours?' The question was delicately put, great attention suddenly being paid to his pipe.

Melanie shrugged uneasily. 'I've made up my mind,' she said.

Her father said nothing but an expressive shake of his head said a lot. 'Don't tell Paul about Linda, Dad,' Melanie said at last after a long silence. 'He mustn't know. I don't want him nosing round for an exclusive.'

'More secrets, eh? I'll do my best.' He smiled gently. 'Leave your mother to me. I know how to deal with her.'

'No. I'll tell her myself. In my own time,' Melanie said, a heavy tiredness creeping upon her. 'Don't rush me. I want to tell Paul first.'

'Don't you worry. If you don't want to get married yet, then nobody's going to make you.'

'Thanks, Dad.' A sudden surge of fondness for him swelled within her and impulsively she went across and kissed the top of his balding head, smelling the familiar faint tobacco smell.

'We'll have none of that,' he said, pleased.

★   ★   ★

Her mother had had her hair done. It was the same coppery colour as Melanie's although helped a little now by the hairdresser. They dutifully admired the new shorter style. 'What an

48

afternoon! I met Lorna Kirkbride for coffee and she told me the awful news.'

'What awful news?' Melanie asked, exchanging an anxious glance with her father. How could they know already?

Her mother paused dramatically. 'Frances . . . ' she said in a doom-laden voice. 'Frances has got herself pregnant.'

Melanie managed a nervous smile. 'That's not the end of the world,' she said. 'She is married, Mum, she's quite entitled to have a baby.'

'Yes, but she knows the wedding is booked. We'll have to get someone else. I refuse to have an eight-months-pregnant matron of honour waddling down the aisle after you.'

Melanie and her father laughed, getting a most disapproving look in return. 'And another thing,' her mother continued huffily. 'Where did you get to today? Paul rang and I felt such a fool when I had to say I didn't know where you were. Well?' She softened the question with a smile, still preening her heavily lacquered hair.

'Shall we start tea?' Melanie said brightly, evading the question with practised skill.

As she had known, her mother was happier as she busied herself in the kitchen. She seemed to have temporarily abandoned finding out where Melanie had spent her day but something was still worrying her and she eyed Melanie anxiously. 'You treat that poor man of yours quite dreadfully,' she said. 'He's such a dear and you're almost offhand with him at times. Anyone would think you didn't want to be married.'

It was a heaven-sent opportunity and Melanie did not flinch. 'I don't think I do,' she said distinctly.

It was enough to make her mother pause briefly, her hands submerged in soapy water at the sink. Only briefly. 'Silly girl,' she said. 'I've told you it's simply pre-wedding nerves. All brides suffer from them, believe me. Even I did.' She lowered her voice conspiratorially. 'The night before I married your father, I agonized over whether I was doing the right thing. And I was only eighteen.' Her embarrassment was obvious. 'Your father's the only man I've ever known in *that* way,' she added softly. 'You're older, love, you've had other boyfriends. You're getting yourself into a state about nothing. You're very lucky to have Paul.'

'Mother, I ... we have to talk,' Melanie said firmly. 'I must ... '

'Not now, love, I haven't time.' She glanced at the clock. 'And you haven't much time either. Isn't Paul coming round for you? He said something about dinner with Rob and Annette. What are you going to wear?' She caught sight of Melanie's expression. 'What *is* the matter with you? You're not sickening for that flu bug, are you?'

It was not the right moment to talk. Would it ever be? She would tell Paul tonight and then face up to her mother.

She felt a little guilty for telling her father first before Paul but she had needed his reassurance. Saying she had to get ready, she escaped her mother's frown and hurried upstairs. Why was life so complicated? If she was honest with herself, she had always had a lingering doubt about Paul. His over-confidence frequently irritated her, his impatience always annoyed her. Oh, he could switch on the charm with ease, especially with the older ladies like her mother.

There were gentle moments, how-ever, and she held on to them grimly. Once they were married, it would be fine. As if being married would somehow change him. And her.

With an enormous sigh, she stepped into the comfort of a warm, bubbly bath. She closed her eyes. She would tell him tonight. After dinner. He would understand. Wouldn't he?

★　★　★

They were alone at last. It had been a fraught evening although Rob and Annette were so caught up in each other that they didn't seem to notice the cool atmosphere circulating around Paul and Melanie.

'I don't know what you think you're playing at,' he said harshly as he poured them a late-night drink. 'Swanning off without saying where you're going. It's damned odd behaviour. Your mother was quite worried. Where the hell were you?'

She took the drink from him. Frowning. 'You needn't be so aggressive,' she said quietly. 'I was going to tell you. I couldn't tell you with Rob and Annette around, could I?' She looked for some sign of softening in his expression but there was none. 'Promise you won't be angry,' she murmured, instantly irritated at how juvenile that sounded. 'I've been for an interview for a job,' she continued, trying for nonchalance by sipping her wine, and nearly choking on it. 'I didn't intend to be secretive,' she went on as her coughing subsided. 'But there seemed to be no point in mentioning it as I didn't think I'd a hope of getting it. But I have.'

Paul leapt up, tearing at his tie and loosening it. 'Why, for God's sake? What the hell are you thinking about? Haven't you enough to do with arrangements for the wedding? You can do without settling into a new job. What's wrong with the job at Johnson's?'

'Let me explain. Sit down,' Melanie said, patting the sofa beside her and trying to give him an encouraging smile. But it seemed her news had agitated him too much. 'The job's not here,' she went on, hearing her words singing into a sudden silence. 'It's in the country. A live-in job for about a year.'

'What?' His face was tight with rage, frightening her. 'How can you have a live-in job? You're marrying me. Have you gone crazy?'

'No.' Melanie replaced her glass on the low table before her. 'Please listen. About the wedding ... I'm just not sure any more. I need time. A year. It's not long, is it? I want to think about things. I don't want to make a dreadful mistake. And I can't think about things with you all breathing down my neck.' She looked away. 'Please try to understand. I think I love you ... '

His laugh was harsh, without humour, his eyes glittering with an emotion she did not wish to see. 'Like hell you do,' he hissed. 'If you loved me, you wouldn't put me through this. Damn you, Melanie.' He was beside her and pulled her roughly to her feet, gripping her arms tightly, shaking her. She struggled in his arms, horrified at this reaction.

'Let me go,' she cried. 'You're hurting me!' She twisted her face away from his hot whisky breath as he tried to force a kiss on her. 'Stop it, Paul.'

'Stop it, Paul,' he mimicked horribly, his face looming over hers. 'We'll be married as planned,' he said, dangerously quiet. 'You can put this daft idea of yours right out of your head. You're going to be my wife. Do you hear?'

Melanie shrank back. 'Let me go,' she repeated steadily and, after a long moment, he did just that, so abruptly that she fell back onto the sofa. Ruefully she rubbed her bruised arms, not daring, not wanting, to look at him.

'I'm going,' she said with as much dignity as she could muster. 'I should have known you'd be like this. You didn't even give me the chance to explain properly.' She pulled the ring off her finger and held it silently towards him. His eyes were cold. A stranger's eyes. But he hadn't finished yet.

'One thing before you go,' he said, snatching the ring. 'I don't take treatment like this from anyone, especially not from a little mouse like you. I'll be a laughing-stock and I won't have that. I always thought you were a frigid bitch and now you've proved it. Get out!'

Her eyes were swimming with tears by the time she reached the street. She would have to walk home she realized stupidly, as she hadn't enough on her for a taxi fare. He had behaved predictably enough. Hadn't he? Hadn't she known, deep down, that he would do and say precisely what he had done and said?

However had she imagined herself to be in love with a man like that? All the gentle times had been wiped away tonight. She would remember him always as he had looked just now. Blazingly angry.

Her footsteps were loud on the glistening pavement as she walked away.

3

For the second time, Melanie drove up to Headmoor Hall but this time the sun was shining unhindered out of a clear blue sky which, under the circumstances, was just as well. She was feeling very fragile. Her father had just about prevented a complete break with her mother but their mother/daughter relationship, never close, was strained. Melanie had never seen her mother so angry. She had quite simply taken Paul's side and nothing Melanie could say or do could change her opinion that Paul was being treated very badly. How could Melanie do this to him? The poor man was quite demented. How dare she break his heart? And how was she to explain it to everyone? It made her look such a fool! Some of Paul's family had been planning to come over from Australia and had been so looking forward to it. Couldn't she see that she had spoilt things for everyone with her silliness. She was being completely selfish. It went on and on and on.

In her mother's eyes, Paul was an amusing, charming, confident, good-looking man with prospects. It was a waste of time explaining that under-neath all that a violence simmered that frightened her. Melanie shivered sud-denly as she recalled the eruption of it on that last night together.

She gave a deep shuddering breath as she stopped the car, gripping the wheel tightly and closing her eyes. Tears were never far away these days and, if only it had been possible, how wonderful it would have been to make everyone smile again.

Instead she had suffered a chilling combination of angry outbursts and stony silences, with only her father offering any crumbs of comfort. He loved her. They had had a long chat and he had admitted that perhaps it was for the best. Best she find out now than later, with all the messiness a divorce would involve. As she had suspected, he had never been convinced that she and Paul were right for each other. Two halves of a whole that didn't quite fit, he had muttered, puffing furiously at his pipe, his whole face reddening. She had never realized that he was a romantic at heart. She wondered, not for the first time, why he had married her mother. Her mother was naturally abrasive and her father deserved some-one gentler. And yet they seemed content enough and occasionally a certain look would pass between them that excluded her.

She blinked the tears away and stepped resolutely out into a pleasant warmth. It was country quiet, the air sweet and clean, fresh from its giddy descent from the fells. And there was Linda, waiting informally on the steps, shading her eyes from the sun, dressed in a cerise silk jumpsuit nipped in at the waist with a broad silver belt, and high-heeled silver sandals. A real country girl!

'Welcome back, Melanie,' she said, grasping her hand excitedly. 'It's lovely to see you.' The green eyes were shrewd in a quick assessment. 'You look tired. Quite pale. How are things with you and Paul?'

'Fine.' Melanie flashed a bright smile. She had decided on the way up that there was no point in depressing Linda as well as herself. It was hardly fair on a woman who was coping bravely with her recent bereavement. 'Paul understood. He's happy to give me a little time to think things over,' she said, surprised at how easy it was to lie. She saw Linda's eyes light briefly on her ringless hands. 'I don't wear a ring,' she explained with a smile. 'We put the money in the bank instead.'

'Oh, you poor thing, how utterly business-like and sensible,' Linda said with a wicked smile. 'Thank goodness I've never had to watch the pennies. It must be so boring. Still, I'm glad everything's worked out for you. I told you he would understand if he loved you.' She twirled a waist-length silver chain absently. 'I've arranged for coffee to be sent up to your room. I thought you might want to unpack and put your feet up for a while.'

'That sounds marvellous,' Melanie said, massaging her neck muscles. 'It was a harrowing journey. The motorway was really busy and the road over the moors is so narrow and twisty.'

'You must have a rest.' Linda glanced at her watch. 'I'll see you back down here at . . . let's say two o'clock.' She was clicking her way over the elegant black and white tiled floor as she spoke. 'I'm having a dinner-party tonight. A few friends. Some people will say it's too soon but Philip wouldn't have minded in the least. He used to say that as long as I was happy, he didn't give a hoot about anyone else.' There was a sudden awkward silence and she turned her face away.

From the dining-room came the

sound of voices interspersed with laughter. 'Flowers? Would you like to do the flowers?' The question cut through the silence and Linda was herself again, flinging the words brightly over her shoulder. 'I usually like to do them myself as I find it so relaxing. But today I've a million and one other things to do and several of the guests are staying over so we've got guest-rooms to prepare. Go and unpack first and have your coffee and sandwiches. I'll put the flowers out for you.'

With her knowledge of flower-arranging about nil that was something of a threat. Hoping she wouldn't make too much of a hash of it, Melanie went upstairs to her room where her suitcases were already waiting. She paused a moment just inside the door, letting the calm atmosphere of the pretty room wash over her. Then, ignoring her suitcases, she had her coffee and sandwiches, forcing herself to relax, breathing deeply, thinking only pleasant thoughts.

Mr Johnson had been so understanding, such a dear, as she might have known. He had wished her well on behalf of himself and his dear wife whom she had never met, and had shrugged off the difficulties her leaving would entail. He had made a touching little farewell speech that had moved her to tears and they had presented her with a set of wineglasses and a small cheque. The new girl was already installed, a cheerful, bright girl, but she had an awful lot to learn about the job. So convinced was Melanie that things would go hopelessly wrong that she had left her forwarding address. She had felt a moment's doubt, for Paul was not above snooping around, but she had told herself she must not be paranoid about him.

Melanie smiled now as she finished her coffee. It would be all right. Things seemed black but it would be all right. She put her coffee-cup aside and started reluctantly on the unpacking.

She had precious few clothes. In

anticipation of her forthcoming marriage and changed status as Paul's wife, she had discarded many old well-loved ones, reducing her wardrobe by a good half. They intended that she should continue her career and whilst Melanie had been completely in favour of that, she had worried when Paul had always evaded the subject of children. Once again, she had determined that when they were married, things would be different. Children certainly had a place in her plans, someday.

She saw her wardrobe, what there was of it, afresh as she deposited it amongst the pine drawers and into the huge wardrobe. She would have to get a new dress for evening wear. The red one had been a mistake. Paul's choice. She never normally wore red. Red was such a look-at-me colour and this dress clung sensually to every curve, the neckline dipping to danger-point.

When she had unpacked, she opened the window wide and stepped onto the balcony, breathing in the heady air. Oh, she would be so happy here! The difficulties of the past month were already fading and assuming a lot less importance. Paul had said things in the heat of the moment and she still half expected an apology. She would accept it gracefully, she had decided, but there would be no going back. It was over. What hurt most was that there had been no mention of his sorrow at losing her.

She saw now how shallow his so-called love for her had been. No mention of how much he loved and needed her. Nothing. If only he had taken her in his arms and told her that. Perhaps it might have been different. If only . . .

But she was forgetting Conrad and this absurd infatuation she seemed to have developed for him. He was a complete stranger for heaven's sake, and just now her heart had skipped a beat when she had mistakenly thought she saw him coming across the lawns towards her. She had thought she had conquered that silly feeling, thought it had been something to do with the euphoria of getting the job, but she realized now that it was still as strong as ever. What was the matter with her? He was a perfectly ordinary man; a very nice man, but quite ordinary, and she really had to pull herself together before she made a complete fool of herself.

Oh heavens, it was nearly time to begin the flower-arranging. Linda had given her no opportunity to explain that flower-arranging was not her forte. Normally she was happy enough to dump a bunch of fresh flowers unceremoniously in a vase and leave it at that. If she was feeling artistic, she might add a few pieces of fern. It would seem, judging by the elaborate arrangements all over the house, that Linda would require something a little more than that.

In the dining-room, two girls were engaged in making the room and table attractive. Not that they needed to work very hard at it, for it was indeed a beautiful room of deepest red and gleaming mahogany. A magnificent marble fireplace fought for attention with the violent seascape hanging above it.

Linda introduced her and told them she was going to do the flowers. The girls smiled at her, eyeing her up and down swiftly, before resuming the dusting and polishing. Linda whirled back to face her, a little worried frown on her face. 'There's so much still to do. I really don't know how I'm going to fit everything in. Now, where were we? Ah yes, the flowers! There they are, my dear, do what you like with them. You'll find vases in that cupboard. Use whatever you like but do make sure you use the pewter jug for a small arrangement. It's one of my favourites. When you've finished, disperse them round the house. In the hall, on the landings, in the library and in here. All right?'

Somewhat bewildered, Melanie watched the small cerise figure depart, only to return immediately. 'I forgot to tell you that Conrad's offered to take you round the estate when you've finished. Wear sensible shoes, he says.' She laughed and glanced down at Melanie's strappy navy high-heels. 'Do you have any? I do detest sensible shoes, don't you?' And she was finally gone, her decidedly unsensible shoes tapping over the polished parquet floor, the door clicking shut behind her.

The two girls heaved dramatic sighs of relief. 'Lucky you,' one of them said. 'I wish Conrad would show me round the estate. Have you met him?' She grinned at Melanie. She was very young, very tall and very slim. 'He's a bit old for me but he's ever so dishy. Isn't he, Barbara?'

Barbara agreed. 'He reminds me of . . . who is it? You know? He's on the telly . . . in that programme. What is it?'

The other girl laughed. 'Shut up. Let her get on with the flowers. It's going to take her all afternoon to sort that lot out.'

Looking at them, Melanie was inclined to agree. There were masses of cut blooms fresh from the garden, feathery greenery and a selection of chunkier, darker leaves.

Thankfully, the girls were no longer watching her, caught up with removing small ornaments from the top of a tall bureau and carefully dusting them. Melanie took a deep breath and set to work tentatively, not quite sure where to start. Something small for the pewter jug? No, that was too small, it looked ridiculous. Yellow, deep yellow, would look lovely. It wasn't long before she was beginning to enjoy herself. The first arrangement in the pewter jug looked, to her inexperienced eyes, charming. More confident now, she began to sort out the remainder of the flowers and proudly placed them around the house. The final arrangement in the biggest vase would take pride of place on a sideboard in the dining-room where it would be reflected in a handsome mirror.

She picked up the heavy pot vase, turned and found herself confronted by a solid, bulky male presence, managing by the sheerest good fortune to keep hold of the vase and its scented contents.

'Do you make a habit of bumping into people?' Conrad asked with a laugh as he gently pushed her away.

'Just you,' she said, trying to keep her voice light and pretending to examine the flowers to hide a blush. 'It's your fault. You keep creeping up on me.'

He grinned. 'Have you finished yet?'

'Just about.' She placed the vase in position, hand shaking a little, and screwed up her face as she looked at it. 'What do you think?' she asked. 'Have I overdone it?'

'No, it's fine,' he said dismissively and a little impatiently. He glanced over to the two girls who were suddenly very busy and then back to her, lowering his voice. 'You shouldn't be cooped up in here,' he said. 'I thought we might take a walk down to the river. We might as

71

well enjoy the sunshine.'

'I'd like that,' she said, smiling at him, more in control now. 'Give me ten minutes and I'll be ready.'

'Okay. I'll be outside on the terrace.'

She fiddled a moment unnecessarily with the flowers when he had gone, aware of the whispers and giggles behind her, trying to ignore the racing of her pulse. Her body was behaving in an extraordinary way, totally separate from her more sensible mind which seemed to be looking on in amazement and amusement. Never before had a man had this effect on her. Paul certainly had not. Her senses had always remained firmly reined in with Paul, and she was perceptive enough to know that it was her coolness and faint lack of interest that had attracted him. He had never had to work very hard with his women and she had represented something of a challenge.

'Have a nice walk,' Barbara said coyly as she made to leave. 'Who knows what he might try once he gets you down by the river?'

Smiling with them, she hurried to get ready, stepping briskly out of her suit and rummaging for jeans and a blouse. Ten minutes! Ten minutes was no time at all. Why on earth had she specified so short a time, giving herself no chance to fuss with her appearance as she would have liked to do. She hastily brushed her hair, tied it back with a narrow black ribbon, tucked the blouse into the waistband of her jeans, added a belt and was ready.

'Good timing,' he said appreciatively as she walked round the flagged terrace to where he was waiting. 'When you said ten minutes, I thought you meant a woman's ten minutes.'

'Pig!' she said, joining in his laugh as they set off down the first flight of wide, stone steps. Impressive stone urns held tumbling cascades of soft colour, huge clumps of rose-pink flowers spilled gloriously onto the steps and a hedge of lavender fringed the lower rockery. At the foot of the steps, manicured lawns sloped towards rougher pasture grass through which a narrow path meandered.

River sounds met them as they approached the path. Melanie glanced back at the house, the sombre grey stone softened by creeping ivy, her balcony clearly visible. 'It's lovely here,' she said softly. 'The air's so clean. So fresh. I feel I want to take deep breaths all the time.'

He said nothing but she knew he somehow approved of her comment. 'I'm glad you're back,' he said at last, almost to himself. 'I've been looking forward to seeing you again.'

'Have you?' She found herself ridiculously pleased at the casual remark. 'I'm glad to be back,' she said firmly. 'Things have been a bit awkward. I used to work for an engineering company, just a small firm, and it's been a trial working out my notice. Everyone was very understanding but Mr Johnson . . . he was my boss . . . he's been ill recently and the company's going through a bad patch and . . . ' she pasued, remembering. 'I can't help but feel guilty at leaving. The new girl won't really be able to cope properly for quite some time.'

'You shouldn't feel guilty,' he said. 'There's never a right time to leave. If I left Headmoor now, for instance, I'd be leaving Linda just when she's extra dependent on me. She doesn't know much about running the estate. Philip took an interest in that side of things. He didn't interfere but he liked to know what was going on, whether the tenants had any problems, that sort of thing. Just thinking of leaving makes me feel hellish guilty but this job, this new job, won't be open for ever. Bob's been patient enough as it is. I've got to decide by the fall anyway.' He gave a small sigh. 'I should just pack up and go. Helen will be well enough by then. I don't know why I'm hesitating.' He shot her a quick sideways glance. 'What about you, would you have the nerve to uproot yourself completely?'

'And move to America, you mean?' Melanie smiled, the casual mention of Helen disturbing her. It seemed that, if he went, she was going too. She considered his question. 'I'm not sure,' she said at last. 'It's an awfully long way.'

He laughed. 'There are such things as planes,' he said drily. 'Five or six hours and you'd be back here. You wouldn't have to swim the Atlantic.'

She giggled at that, glancing shyly at him. He was still looking enquiringly at her, sun streaking his upper body. He was wearing jeans and an open-necked shirt. There was a glimpse of bare skin and a suggestion of dark hairs nestling there. She had an overwhelming desire to slip deeply into those arms, to be held close, to hear the pounding of his heart against hers. She was now close enough to smell a pleasant male scent.

'Well?'

'Well, what?'

'You weren't listening,' he accused,

the smile not leaving his eyes. 'I asked what you thought of Linda.'

'Did you? Sorry, I was miles away.' She paused thoughtfully. 'Linda? I hardly know her yet. I like her, if that's what you mean. When I told my father I was coming to work for her, he was quite put out. He wanted me to think about it very carefully. I suspect he thought she might be a bad influence. He called her a floozie . . . ' She laughed shortly. 'Of course we weren't around at the time of the scandal or whatever it was.'

'Hard to understand, isn't it? All that fuss! She's had a tough time over the years and that's why she likes to keep Headmoor a secret. She goes to great lengths to make sure nobody knows where it is, except for friends and people she can trust.'

'They could find out, surely, if they wanted to,' Melanie pointed out matter-of-factly. 'I wonder sometimes if she isn't a little bit paranoid about the press.'

He shrugged. 'Can you blame her? According to Jean, she's very bitter about that photograph, the one with Christofer-Jon. If only she'd had a chance to explain to Philip, she says. She worries that he died thinking she had been unfaithful.'

'And had she?' Melanie asked quietly, instantly sorry to have put the question. 'I'm sorry,' she murmured. 'It's just that . . . well, imagine getting yourself photographed with a man like that? He's taking half the models in London out according to the papers. Do you know anything about him, Conrad? How old is he? He seems to have been around for some time, first in Canada and the States and now here.'

'He's older than me,' Conrad said with a grin. 'Forty or thereabouts. You've got to give it to him, he certainly knows how to attract the ladies.'

'I suppose it could all have been perfectly innocent,' Melanie mused thoughtfully. 'What do you think? You know Linda better than I do.'

'I think we're gossiping,' he said with mock indignation. 'Who started this?'

'You did,' Melanie reminded him. 'I'm just curious, that's all. And remember, Conrad, I've got to work closely with her. I don't like secrets.'

For a moment he looked as if he were about to say something but changed his mind and they reached the end of the path in silence. They had to scramble through untidy shrubbery as the path petered out and at last were on the river bank.

He wasn't going to get away with it as easily as that. Melanie waited until they were on firmer ground before demanding aggressively, 'Are you going to tell me or not?'

'Tell you what?' A grin was maddeningly glued to his face.

'Tell me what you nearly told me back there. Or are you afraid I can't keep a secret? You needn't worry. I can be terribly discreet.'

He looked at her long and hard. 'Now and then they would come up

79

with photographs and rumours,' he began. 'They hurt Linda. Philip had a thick skin but they hurt her. They would talk about parties she had been to in London. Without Philip of course. According to them, she was money mad and had only married Philip for his money and position. It wasn't true. She likes the money of course, but then, given the opportunity, wouldn't you? And she does spend a lot of time in London. But that doesn't mean she's meeting up with younger men when she's there. Or at least . . . ' His voice rose and surprised her in its sudden anger. 'This time I don't know what the hell she's been playing at. He's so obviously after her money, don't you think? How can he be seriously interested in her? And how can she make a fool of herself?'

They were beside the tumbling, silvery stream they called the river and for a moment stood and watched its ever-changing pattern. Melanie's thoughts, as she struggled to understand what he was saying, were suddenly as turbulent as the rushing water and she saw from his face that her anxieties were mirrored in him. 'Tell me,' she whispered, drawing a touch closer, wanting to help. 'You want to tell someone and it might as well be me.'

'Melanie . . . ' He raised troubled eyes. 'I hate to tell you this but it's what happened. They must have been in one of the empty cottages on the estate, spent the afternoon there, although that sort of thing seems a bit sordid for Linda. I saw him leaving, saw her kissing him goodbye.' He picked up a pebble idly and threw it into the stream. 'I couldn't believe it. I just stood there and watched. Thank God, they didn't see me. I honestly couldn't believe it of her. It made me wonder about all those other times. Had she really been deceiving Philip all these years? If so, she made a good job of it. He thought she was an angel.'

'Surely she can be forgiven one mistake,' Melanie said. 'This Christofer-Jon looks to me to be the sort of man who is very good at flattery and all women are susceptible to that.'

'Even you?' He laughed. 'Did anyone tell you how beautiful you are? And that you have a fascinating, husky voice and the most gorgeous eyes I've ever seen. I can't stop looking at you.'

Melanie stiffened. She had learnt over the years how to accept compliments. With a big smile and a murmured thank you. But this was different. Was he serious? Was he teasing?

Despite that, she could not help a sudden glow burning deep within at the words and turned her face away, not daring to look into his eyes, a dryness in her throat. 'It's so quiet here,' she said softly. 'Listen. Just the birds and the water and nothing else. Just silence. You can't even see the house now. It's as if . . .'

'As if we were alone in the world,' he said, surprising her with his sensitivity. It was true. They were alone. Powerfully alone. For a disturbingly long moment, she found her eyes drawn to his, looking away before he did, seeing her own feelings mirrored there. Surely she couldn't be mistaken about a thing like that?

He was the first to break the silence, a silence when millions of unspoken questions filled the air. His voice was strange as he nodded towards the stream. 'It's a tributary of the Tees,' he said. 'There's a footbridge lower down at the farm, or we can use the stepping-stones here. Are you game?'

'Of course.' Melanie laughed, recovering her composure, and grateful for the lighter vein in the conversation. 'I haven't used stepping-stones since I was a little girl,' she added. 'I'll probably fall in.'

He was already holding out his hand and she was eyeing the three or four widely spaced stones with some trepidation. They were flat but slippery and she nearly lost her footing on every one, laughing as she regained her balance precariously, aware of the warm pressure of his hand on hers and the rapid beating of her heart. All around them, the soft summery sounds enveloped them in their little private world. She wanted this moment to go on forever.

He released her hand at once when they were across. She brushed down her jeans, a little confused. His hand had felt so right and the instant letting go deflated her.

'Come on, I might as well show you my cottage. We're nearly there,' he said, adding that he didn't usually reach it by such a tortuous route.

'I don't know why, but I imagine you lived in at the Hall,' Melanie said, pushing at her hair as it fell heavily forward. 'There's so much room there.'

'I did until about a year ago. The cottage was meant for me and Helen. It's a mess, I'm afraid. I don't have much time to sort it out.'

Helen again! Who on earth was this Helen? Obviously his girlfriend. In that case, where was she now and what was this traumatic experience Linda had hinted at? Curiously, Melanie cast a glance his way. She was still thinking of that sweetly long look back there. If Helen was his girlfriend, he had no right to be looking at another woman in *that* way. She felt a moment's irritation towards him. He had a nerve. Perhaps he was in the middle of a divorce. Well he ought to tell her. It was unfair not to, and she was hardly helping with her legs like jelly every time he so much as looked at her. She ought to take a grip on herself, stop this nonsense before it, too, went too far.

'It's a bachelor's hovel,' Conrad warned, laughter in his voice. 'Complete with sink full of dirty dishes and inches of fluff on the carpet.'

'If you've dragged me all the way up here just to do your washing-up, you can think again,' she said lightly. 'I hate washing-up and I'm very bad at it.'

'I'm good at it,' he said. 'When I get round to it, that is. Mrs Harris usually does it for me.'

'Who's Mrs Harris?'

'She's from the village. She comes in a couple of mornings a week to do the odd bit of dusting.'

'Odd bit of dusting indeed.' Melanie sniffed her contempt at that. 'You probably don't appreciate what the poor lady does for you, a mere male like you. Housework is a thankless task. I don't know many women who enjoy it, and why should they?' she added defiantly.

'Hey, steady on!' He grinned. 'Are you one of these modern girls then, intending to pursue your career and let your poor old husband look after the house and the baby?'

'Sort of.' She eyed him suspiciously, not sure if he was teasing her or not. She decided uncomfortably that he was. Her fault for letting the conversation turn serious. 'I believe marriage should be a joint effort,' she continued, reluctant to let the matter drop until she had clarified her views. 'Of course I'd do my share.' She stopped, irritated.

Now she sounded smug and superior and she hadn't meant to.

'Great! I totally agree with you,' he said, with another laugh that she, against her better judgement, joined in with. 'We're nearly there. Close your eyes.'

She did as she was told. As she did so, she felt the shock of his hand once more on hers as he guided her forward up a steep, rough path. Shut off momentarily as she was, his touch had even more impact, sending pleasurable shock waves racing through her veins.

'Careful.' His hand was at her waist, gentle, respectful, and then he was telling her with scarcely concealed boyish delight that she could open her eyes. They were there.

She was unprepared for the beauty of the view now that they had rounded the hill and were looking down on the cottage nestling sleepily amongst trees.

'It's perfect,' she exclaimed after a long, satisfying look. 'It should be called

Rose Cottage, something pretty like that.'

'Hold on a bit. Wait until you get nearer,' he said. 'It's been neglected over the years. We only acquired it last year and I've been doing boring but necessary things like fixing the roof and the damp. That sort of thing doesn't show, does it? That's why it's still scruffy. Sorry about the garden, that'll soon tidy up.' He gave an apologetic smile as they headed down. 'If I'd stayed, I was going to have a real cottage some day. Hollyhocks and herbs by the kitchen window. And old-fashioned roses. Helen likes roses.' He helped her over a stile with another smile. 'You don't get cottage gardens in Vermont. People have a more relaxed attitude to gardening. It's all less fussy. Just big expanses of lawn and a few bushes. And the flag-pole,' he added. 'They like to fly the flag over there.'

'I love cottage gardens,' Melanie said firmly. 'They're so beautiful. They look so disorganized. They're worth all the effort, surely?'

Conrad smiled his agreement. The garden at close quarters was not as bad as he'd made it out to be and there was a profusion of spindly climbers trailing round the white-painted front door. Inside, it was tidy but uninspiring. It was crying out for little feminine touches to bring out its cottagey charm. The simple, stark lines of his furniture needed softening and the small windows needed special treatment to draw attention to them. There were few ornaments and pictures and no flowers.

'Well?' He was waiting for her reaction, a proprietorial look on his face, and she did not want to disappoint him.

'It's ... it's cosy,' she said with a smile.

'Cute, is it?' He laughed. 'That's the last thing it is. Go on, say it, it needs a woman's touch.'

'Well, as you've brought it up, yes. Yes it does,' she said with conviction. 'Here and there,' she added vaguely.

He nodded. 'Fancy a coffee?' he asked. 'I can rustle one up in a few minutes. There might be some clean cups,' he added with a twinkle in his eye.

Melanie peeped into the kitchen and retreated hastily. He was quite right about the mountain of dishes. She left him rummaging for cups and wandered back into the little sitting-room. It needed redecorating. A faded, busy wallpaper competed with an equally busy carpet. Not his choice, she decided, with an authoritative glance at it; probably left over from the previous occupant. A few sporting trophies must be his. They were on a small table together with some photographs. One was of an elderly couple smiling full-face into the camera and the other, silver-framed, was of an unsmiling, fair-haired woman with large, serious eyes. She had the sort of well-structured face that meant she would still be striking in old age. Her blue-grey eyes stared solemnly at Melanie.

She was still holding it when Conrad came through with the coffee. At once, although he almost succeeded in hiding it, an apprehensive look flitted across his face. 'I see you've found Helen,' he said. 'That was taken about two years ago. She's got long hair now.'

Calmly, Melanie replaced it, sensing a fine gossamer veil descending on what had seemed a growing rapport between them. She wished she hadn't picked up the photograph. She didn't want to know about her. About Helen. Dammit, she was beautiful! No wonder he was in love with her.

'Linda said she'd mentioned Helen to you. How much did she tell you?'

'Not much.' She accepted a cup of coffee with a smile. 'Look, it really doesn't matter. You needn't talk about it. I didn't mean to pry. And Linda says it's painful for you to discuss it.'

'Yes, it's still painful, but . . . sometimes it's better to talk,' he said, sitting down opposite her, staring just beyond her, his eyes full of sorrow. 'We were in an accident,' he said quietly, so quietly that she had to strain to hear him. 'A car accident. Winter here on the fells can be treacherous. Snow and packed ice. I should have known better than to let her drive in those conditions.' He paused, an unnatural stillness about him. 'The roads were very icy and she only had a provisional licence.' He managed a wry smile. 'She said she should practise in all conditions and that included icy roads. She said she'd have to get used to them.' He stood up abruptly and crossed over to the window so that she could no longer see his face, although the depth of his emotion was quite clearly reflected in his voice. 'The bend was too sharp and we skidded. It all happened so quickly and she couldn't control it. I suppose an experienced driver might just have . . . she was wearing the sort of shoes you wear and they gave her no chance. As we started to skid, I yelled out for her to turn into it, not to fight it. I heard her cry out . . . ' He paused, giving a deep sigh, the words spilling out in his anxiety. 'There was a truck heading towards us. We were on the wrong side of the road by now. I tell you, Melanie, I've never been so frightened in my life. I thought that was it. We must have missed it but ended up in the stone wall at the side of the road. The next minute we were being lifted out. At least, it seemed like the next minute. It must have taken some time for the ambulance and fire brigade to get up. It took them a long time to get Helen out. I was just dazed but she was hurt. Badly.

'It was touch and go at first but she's a fighter and she had something to fight for. The wedding's booked and I told her we wouldn't postpone it so she'd better get herself fit for that. I think that's what's kept her going, given her the will to live. I was beside her constantly during those first few days.'

'How is she now?' Melanie asked, her

mouth dry, reeling from his words.

'Better. She's still in hospital in Newcastle.' He returned to his chair and smiled at her, a little shakily. 'It still upsets me, talking about it.' He sipped his coffee, his smile more steady, 'I get over as often as I can. You must come with me sometime. She loves to have visitors. Now that she's getting better, she's bored.' He drained his coffee and set the cup down. 'She won't have it that I'm to blame.'

'How could you be?' Melanie said quickly. 'Anyone can skid on black ice. I could. You could. It was just an accident.' She finished her coffee too and stood up, tugging down her blouse in a nervous gesture. 'If you don't mind, Conrad, I'd like to get back. Linda might want me for something.' Her disappointment at his involvement with Helen was so intense that she felt sick and had to fight against a most unreasonable and shameful dislike of the girl lying bravely in a hospital bed. He loved her and it was appalling that

94

she should think such thoughts.

They walked back — along the lane, which was quicker, and Melanie carefully kept her distance as if Helen could somehow see them. She was aware that she was guilty of flirting with him this afternoon but he was not entirely blameless. For a moment back there, the barrier had been broken down. For a moment back there, something had happened between them and that could never be erased.

'I hate dinner-parties,' he said, breaking a silence that was no longer comfortable. 'Stiff shirt, tie, small-talk. Have you something decent to wear? In this house, they dress up for parties.'

'But . . . am I invited?' Melanie asked in surprise. 'She said it was for a few friends and I'm hardly that.'

'No, you're staff,' he said roughly. 'So am I. It makes it awkward, particularly as there are some of her friends who won't hesitate to remind you. Stick by me if you like. Peasants together.' He grinned suddenly, the first smile for some time, and with an effort she managed a weak reply.

He left her at the Hall and she stood for a while, letting the sun soothe her, feeling the tears pricking once more. In the last few weeks she had made a real mess of her life, of her future. Materially, marriage with Paul would have been comfortable. Paul liked his comforts. Lots of girls would give their all for that. Would she have been able to ignore the casual affairs that Paul's set seemed to be constantly engaged in or was that just talk? Paul had put forward the idea that a casual affair, now and then, spiced up a marriage, and had laughed at her horrified reaction, accusing her of being old-fashioned and strait-laced.

Was she old-fashioned? How awful to be accused of that. Oh, damn Paul! And damn Conrad too! She had to pull herself together, stop wallowing in self-pity, stop thinking of Conrad as a lover. He must be a friend. Nothing more.

She bit her lip in sudden anguish as a sudden vision of his face appeared. He wasn't so classically handsome as Paul, was he? Despite the sun, a chill caught at her and she hugged herself. Already she knew every inch of his face, every line. Already she was recognizing the moment just before he smiled. Already she could sense his change of moods. And those eyes! She wanted to drown in the depths of them, wanted him to look at her again in *that* way. That special look that passes between lovers.

She was alone on the terrace. She took one final glance at the sunny splendour of the gardens and went indoors to find Linda.

4

She found her entrenched in the conservatory, silver sandals kicked off and her feet up. She looked up and smiled as Melanie came in.

'Preparations are complete,' she said happily. 'Guest-rooms ready. A most marvellous meal planned. Jean is up to her eyes in pastry in the kitchen. It's an age since I last entertained, I'm so looking forward to it.' She took in Melanie's tousled appearance. 'So, Conrad managed to drag you out, did he? Did you enjoy your walk?'

Melanie nodded, settling herself on the wide window-seat, the sun warm on her back. She looked round the room with pleasure. Sparkling white tiled floor, cool cane furniture, pretty flow-ered drapes to keep off the glare, and plants crammed everywhere. It was a happy room and it was a relief to feel some small happiness creeping back to her after the depression that had ended her walk.

'It's lovely down by the river,' she said chattily. 'Conrad took me to see his cottage.'

'Ah, the cottage!' Linda sighed, putting down the glossy fashion magazine she had been leafing through. 'Isn't it just too perfect? Or at least it will be when it's finished. Roses round the door, beamed ceiling, a heaven of a garden for children to play in. Perfect. What more could anyone ask? Of course if he had his way, he'd give it all up. Don't you agree that it's high time he forgot this ridiculous notion of finding his roots or whatever. I hope you told him that he's quite mad to consider leaving all this for some dubious venture in New England.'

'I don't know him well enough to tell him what to do,' Melanie pointed out reasonably. 'And he seems set on the idea. You know all about the job then?'

'Oh yes.' Linda dismissed it airily. 'I

know exactly where it is. Lovely spot. A bit like the English Lakes really. I've met the prospective partner too, a real go-getting young man. As a business venture I suppose it will do well, but is it the right thing for Conrad?' She smiled a gentle smile. 'It's pure nostalgia on his part. He has rose-coloured spectacles, I'm afraid. Haven't you heard him waxing lyrical about the New England fall? No, I'm afraid, he's not using his head. He hasn't considered the negative aspects of it.'

'What are they?' Melanie asked, puzzled. 'It sounds just right for him. He loves Vermont. He gets on well with whoever it is he's going into business with. And he loves the outdoors, the hills, the space.'

Linda sniffed. 'What do you call that out there?' She waved vaguely towards the window. 'Hills. Space. It's just the same.' She looked thoughtfully at Melanie. 'You think I'm being selfish, don't you? And I suppose I am. Of course he must go if he wants to. I did think when I persuaded him to take on the cottage that he would forget it. It's such an olde-worlde place that I thought it might make him change his mind. I hoped Helen would fall in love with it, and if anyone can make him change his mind, surely she can. But . . . ' She gave an exaggerated sigh. 'Silly of me. It'll be such a bore looking for a new man. Conrad keeps things running so smoothly. If there are problems, I'm never aware of them.'

'What does Helen think about it? About going to America?' Melanie asked, aware that her voice sounded a little odd and hoping Linda would not notice.

'Helen? Oh, he's been telling you about that, has he?'

'Yes. He told me all about it,' Melanie said. 'He feels very badly about it too. Very upset.'

Linda glanced at her sharply. 'Helen will come through it all right,' he said. 'As for America, I really have no idea what she thinks. Presumably she's happy enough about it. She doesn't have a lot of choice, does she? If he's made up his mind, then . . . '

'Oh, I don't agree,' Melanie interrupted. 'Why should she go if she doesn't want to? A woman nowadays doesn't have to follow her man to the ends of the earth. That's quite outdated.'

'Is it?' Linda's smile broadened. 'It depends on the man, my dear. And the woman. Personally I would have followed my Philip into darkest Africa if he'd wanted me to.'

Melanie fell silent. Maybe that was what was wrong with her and Paul. She wasn't even sure she would have followed him down to London. However, Linda's servile attitude irritated her. She fidgeted a little on the wide seat, fingering the fronds of a feathery palm nearby as Linda, her smile intact, continued.

'Helen's a difficult girl. Quiet. One of those people who keep their feelings well hidden. Conrad's asked me several times to visit her in hospital but so far I've managed to avoid it. I hate hospitals. And I wouldn't know what to say to her.' She grimaced. 'I know. Tell me I'm being selfish again.'

'Not a bit.' Melanie smiled sympathetically. 'I don't like hospitals either. He's asked me to go to see her as well, but I don't intend to either.'

They exchanged a guilty smile. Melanie would have liked to probe deeper into the relationship between Conrad and Helen but it seemed the wrong moment to do so as Linda shifted in her chair in a deliberate attempt to relax.

'You'll enjoy dinner tonight,' she said after a moment, her eyes closed. 'Jean's a good cook. Simple, very fresh fare is our speciality here. Just the thing my guests expect. We grow all our own fruit and vegetables and Jean makes jams and pickles and chutneys. It's all a complete mystery to me.'

From her seat by the window, Melanie frowned. So, Conrad was right.

She was expected for dinner. What should she wear? Would a brightly patterned cotton skirt and plain top be posh enough or would she look too much like the hired help in it? That only left the red dress. Was there some way she could damp down its effect? Her frown deepened. Short of wearing a cardigan over it, that idea was ludicrous. It was a dress that liked to speak its mind.

'The flowers were lovely by the way. Thank you,' Linda said dreamily, the constant tapping of her fingers against the chair belying her relaxed posture. 'Unconventional but charming.'

'I'm glad you liked them,' Melanie said absent-mindedly, still considering the vexed problem of a dress.

'Have you brought an evening dress?' Linda suddenly asked, as if reading her mind. She abandoned her attempts at relaxation and sat up in the chair, blinking at the bright sunlight. 'We do dress up rather. Philip insisted. Even when there was only the two of us, we always dressed for dinner. He was a stickler for detail and he was a man who always wore his clothes so well.' She laughed, sadness in her eyes. 'You have style too, my dear, in your own way. You're always most attractively presented.'

'I do have an evening dress,' Melanie began doubtfully, hardly hearing Linda, her thoughts still on the touchy subject of what to wear. 'Although I . . .'

'Don't worry,' Linda interrupted with a kind smile. 'I suspected you might not be prepared so I've arranged for several of mine to be left in your room. Feel free to wear whichever you like best.' She took in Melanie's ruffled appearance afresh, patting her own hair self-consciously. 'If you don't mind my saying so, your hair is in need of a trim. I must introduce you to my hairdresser. He's a darling man and quite the best around.'

Surely Linda couldn't mean . . . ?

Linda gave a soft giggle. 'I know what you're thinking,' she said. 'The power of the press, eh? My hairdresser's called Michael and he runs this marvellous salon in Newcastle. We keep him to ourselves. We don't want him moving to London. There's far too much competition down there. Christofer-Jon is merely an acquaintance, Melanie. That photograph was most misleading.'

How could she say that after what Conrad had said this afternoon? And why did she think it necessary to offer an explanation? Guilt? Aware that she was blushing, Melanie tugged ineffectually at the ribbon that anchored her hair. 'Thank you for the dresses,' she said with a grateful smile. 'It was kind of you. I do have one with me as I said, but it's . . . well, I don't feel very comfortable in it.'

'They may not fit.' Linda eyed her doubtfully. 'I bought them all quite recently to cheer myself up after Philip died. I must have lost weight. The worry and everything I expect.' She sighed, managing a sad smile. 'Philip hated me to go through what he called my thin phases. Men like their women a little rounded. We never learn, do we?' She stretched and reached for her shoes, slipping them onto dainty feet. 'I'm hoping Jean's cooking will soon pile the pounds on. She's a great believer in cream with everything. So was Philip, and that was entirely against doctor's orders.'

* * *

After a long, leisurely bath where she tried, not entirely satisfactorily, to empty her mind of all her problems, she examined the dresses thrown casually over the bed.

One, in particular, caught her eye. It was exquisite. Silver-grey, with a beaded bodice and softly pleated skirt. She struggled into it, willing it to fit, but admitting defeat when the zip refused to budge. If she breathed in, she might get it to fasten. Just. But, no, she couldn't take the chance of breaking it, not such an expensive dress. None of the others fitted either. They were all beautifully cut and silky materials that she slid her hands over lovingly, but it was no use. She cast them aside reluctantly.

So, she would either have to go down-market with a skirt and top or wear the red dress. She really had no choice. She had no intention of looking like the poor relation. With a sigh, she dragged the dress from the wardrobe. She could already sense people arriving. Cars. Laughter. The bell ringing. Linda's excited voice. She could not spend any longer dithering.

She slipped into minuscule lacy white underwear. Brand-new, she had bought it as the first item in her trousseau. Now, of course, there was no point in keeping it. It gave her courage because it looked so pretty. Now for the dress itself! There were a lot of memories associated with it that she preferred to forget. Just looking at herself brought them flooding back instantly.

It was a scarlet second skin, moulding itself to every curve, every hollow, the material caressing her body as boldly as a lover. She surveyed herself through half-closed eyes. Paul had declared it to be a knock-out. It ought to have clashed alarmingly with her hair but somehow it did not. The effect was unusual. What on earth was she worrying about? It was an adult dinner-party she was going to, not a children's birthday treat.

Time to go down and she was nervous. She had no intention, either, of clinging to Conrad all evening as he had light-heartedly suggested. She was sure she would find Linda's friends interesting and surely not so petty as to mind that she was 'staff'.

Mellow music drifted from the direction of the library where pre-dinner drinks were in progress. Melanie came softly down the deeply carpeted stairs, inhaling her own floral perfume, smoothing down her dress, pausing where the stairs turned and taking a deep, steadying breath. Below her, a woman in pale blue, crossing the hall, glanced up at her and smiled. 'Good evening,' she said. 'You must be the PA. Linda's told me all about you. Do come down, there's no need to cower on the stairs.'

Annoyed that she should be accused of cowering, Melanie came slowly down. The woman was a great deal taller than herself, in her early fifties, with a clear skin and dark hair shot through quite attractively with grey. She introduced herself as Polly Richards, the local GP's wife. Her handshake was firm and warm, her eyes friendly. Melanie liked her and even forgave her the 'cowering'. Entering the library at her side made the difficult moment a little easier. There was no sign of Linda or Conrad, just the usual bewildering mix of strange faces and high-pitched, unnatural laughter. The company was, without exception, beautifully turned out, and Melanie was thankful she had not opted for the skirt and top.

George Richards was a balding man with worried eyes. Left alone with him, Melanie discovered that he, too, disliked small-talk. In a brief conversation, he gave her a potted history of himself, of Polly, and of their grown-up children, divulging the information in an amusingly earnest manner. Melanie liked him, felt perfectly at ease with him, and they were getting on so well that it was a pity they were forced to circulate.

Melanie was drawn towards a woman of about her own age, wearing a fussy, frilled, off-the-shoulder gown in orange taffeta. The look on her face was sullen, but that could be because she was temporarily alone, presumably abandoned by her escort.

'I'm Kate,' she said as Melanie introduced herself. 'I've come with Ben.' She pointed out a straggly beanpole of a man with an untidy gingery beard. 'Ghastly, isn't he?' She giggled. 'They say looks aren't everything, but I ask you?' She leaned forward conspiratorially. 'He's got pots of money and one has to make small sacrifices.' Her grin was disarming. 'Ben's in publishing. We're here to make damned sure that when this awful book's ready, she doesn't hawk it off to somebody else. It'll sell like hot cakes, Ben says.' She eyed Melanie carefully. 'So you're the new secretary. Marilyn, did you say?'

'Melanie,' she corrected with a smile. Although Kate was being perfectly friendly, Melanie's first impression of her was mixed. There was a distinctly sly look in the dark brown eyes.

'Where is Linda?' she enquired of Kate, fixing a smile on her face and accepting a glass of wine from the tray that was doing the rounds.

'Well she isn't slaving over a hot stove,' Kate said with a laugh. 'She won't be down for ages yet. She likes to make an entrance. It's the frustrated actress in her, I expect.' Her smile revealed small, pearly teeth surrounded by carefully applied orange lipstick. Her hair, black, was piled on top of her head in an elegant chignon with a few curly wisps escaping from it. She wore huge emerald earrings and a matching pendant shone against her creamy bare skin. 'Is that one of Linda's dresses you're wearing?' The surprising question was calmly put and Melanie felt herself flush.

'No, my own,' she said quietly, feeling her heart pound with sudden annoyance.

'Oh, my, I've offended you.' Kate gave a loud giggle. 'I'm sorry, but how can you poor working-girls afford things like that?' She examined the dress with a calculated stare. 'It looks like the kind of thing Linda wears.'

'Thank you,' Melanie murmured sweetly. She was learning. Why be intimidated when the woman opposite had more money than tact?

'Well, actually, I meant . . . ' Kate stopped, confused. 'I buy five or six dresses like this every year,' she continued unabashed. 'One has to for the season. I attend so many functions and one dare not be seen too often in the same dress. Actually, darling . . . ' She glanced around but no one seemed to be listening in. 'I'm a kept woman. Isn't that outrageous? Kept, at the moment, by dearest Ben.' Her eyes roamed the room. 'Dull crowd,' she murmured. 'Not a dishy man in sight.'

The display of boredom was amusing. Melanie glanced with interest at the orange taffeta. A designer dress, it must have cost a fortune. Far more than she could ever afford. The red dress had cost a lot by her own standards but was by no means an exclusive model like Kate's.

'So you never met the late Philip?' Kate asked, not allowing her to escape just yet.

'No, I've only heard about him from Linda. He seems to have been a remarkable man.'

'You can say that again,' Kate said with a wide smile that this time reached her eyes and made her altogether fresher and prettier. 'He was twenty-five years older than her, you know. You can hardly blame her for trying out a younger model, can you? What do you make of this Christofer-Jon business? Personally I think they were having an affair. Too bad she got found out.' She scanned the room again. 'I admired Philip for his sheer nerve. What man in his right mind would leave a poor, invalid wife who'd apparently stuck by him through thick and thin to take up with a very young, very dizzy blonde. On the eve of an election or something equally dramatic. Quite bizarre. Killed his chances of winning of course.' She shook her head and the green earrings danced. 'I've never cared much for Linda. If you ask me, darling, all that dizziness is a sham. She was out to get Philip Fletcher-Grant all those years ago and get him she did.'

'She doesn't strike me as particularly dizzy,' Melanie said thoughtfully. 'She's very sensitive and astute I would have said.'

'She's an actress. Or was. A sort of third-rate actress. No wonder Philip was captivated by her. It must have made a change after Eleanor. Eleanor was his first wife. Dull as sticks as well as having lost the use of everything from the waist down. One can hardly blame him under those circumstances. After all he was a full-blooded male.' Calmly she sipped her drink and Melanie thought a little sadly of Eleanor. What was the real story? Put like that, Philip hardly came out of it as the knight in shining armour.

It was high time she circulated. She made a move to go but Kate caught her arm, unwilling to let her captive audience depart so easily. 'And to cap it all,' she continued, delight in her voice, mock-sorrow in her face, 'she went and died on him a week later. According to the papers, she died of a broken heart. So romantic! And ironic, too, judging by Philip's own demise.' She raised her eyebrows and spoke with satisfaction. 'His name was mud from then on. They made Linda out to be a tramp and they've tried to keep her that way ever since. She doesn't help, dressing the way she does. Tartish is putting it mildly.'

Melanie smiled sweetly, taking the late point that Kate considered her dress in exceedingly poor taste but somehow no longer minding. 'I can't help but feel sorry for Linda,' she murmured.

'Oh yes, feel sorry for her. Wallowing in luxury like she does. A villa in France, an apartment in Florida, a mews flat in London as well as Headmoor. Really roughing it, don't you agree? She spends more on a handbag than someone like you would spend on a complete outfit. Even I have to keep a vague check on my spending.' Her voice was becoming raised and a few heads turned questioningly. Melanie thought it wise to defuse the potentially embarrassing situation by changing the subject. But what to say?

'Do you live locally?' she asked in

desperation, digging deep for the small-talk. It was almost as bad an attempt as 'Do you come here often?'.

'You must be joking.' Kate laughed. Her cheeks were flushed, her dark eyes glittering. 'We certainly do not. We share a flat in London. I potter a little in interior design. Commissions for friends mainly. I have an eye for colour.' She lowered her voice in an ineffective stage-whisper. 'Have you noticed that there's this ghastly pink everywhere here? Wishy-washy if you ask me.'

'An interior designer!' Melanie picked up on the point of interest. 'I've always wanted to meet an interior designer. It's always surprised me what different designers can do to the same room. It's all a matter of taste, isn't it?'

'Absolutely, darling!' Kate eyed her a little suspiciously, uncertain if Melanie were laughing at her. 'You look so utterly practical, darling. I'd die of boredom doing what you — ' She paused, looking suddenly beyond Melanie towards the door. Her eyes had developed an interested look and Melanie discreetly turned to see who had caught her attention.

'Well, if it isn't Conrad Bailes,' Kate whispered as if to herself. 'Have you met him yet? He's fearfully attractive. I'd forgotten how much.' She laughed shortly. 'Of course I know I'm not available, strictly speaking, but . . . ' She glanced towards Ben who was deep in conversation with an elderly man. 'To hell with it! All's fair in love and war.' She smiled prettily, tilting her head in what she obviously thought was a beguiling manner. 'You shouldn't wear red, darling,' she said. 'Not with your colour of hair. I do hope you don't mind me pointing it out but it really jars on someone with an artistic temperament.' She played with the pendant that lay between the soft moulds of her breasts. 'It must be so difficult for you finding things that don't clash with your colouring. I'm lucky. I can wear absolutely anything.'

It was with relief that Melanie

watched her finally depart, taffeta skirt rustling, body swaying, towards a now disgruntled-looking Ben.

'I see you've met Kate.' Conrad was suddenly at her side, classically smart in a black dinner-suit that he wore, despite his protestations, just as easily as if it were his working-clothes. His shirt was sparkling white, emphasizing his tan. 'Sharp tongue, hasn't she?'

Melanie acknowledged his remark with a non-committal smile. She was acutely aware of his steady glance, his half smile. She would be friendly, nothing more. No more flirting. No more *looks*. He was one hundred per cent out of bounds. Nervertheless, she was perversely glad that she was wearing the red siren of a dress.

As she struggled to think of something light-hearted to jiggle the conversation along, Linda made her long-awaited entrance, pausing dramatically just inside the door, smiling, until all heads turned. Her dress was a simple black one, showing off to best advantage the glittering diamond choker at her throat.

'Quite a dress, that!' Conrad murmured as the ripple of small-talk resumed and Linda began to thread her way amongst her guests.

'Yes. Beautiful. She suits black. Blondes do, don't they?'

He laughed. 'I meant yours. You're looking lovely tonight. You should wear that colour more often.'

'Should I?' She smiled, although, deep down, a small irritation was niggling her. How dare he say things like that? An engaged man should damned well behave like one. Especially so, when his fiancée was totally unable to compete. If he didn't stop making remarks like that, she would have to tell him straight.

'You're looking very smart yourself,' she said brightly, aware of the falseness of her smile. 'I don't think we've let the side down.'

'Indeed not.' He twirled the tumbler in his hand, the amber liquid remaining untouched. 'When do you start work with Linda?' he asked.

'The sooner the better.' Melanie relaxed a little. She could cope with general purpose questions like that. 'Although with all these guests, I don't suppose it will be that soon.' She took a sip of wine. 'I never realized how much I enjoyed being busy. There was always masses to do at Johnson's. It was hard work but quite an achievement when I had cleared my in-tray by the end of the day. So far, all I've done here is arrange flowers, go for a walk and I'm about to have dinner. You could hardly call it taxing, could you?'

'You've only just arrived. She's breaking you in gently.' He smiled down at her and she was conscious of and a little amused by the fact that he was trying not very successfully to avoid looking down at her cleavage, straining as it was against the confines of the bodice. 'She'll never get this book of hers finished,' he added roughly. 'Sorry to disappoint you, but it's just an idea that's caught her fancy and Ben Whiteley's pushing her.'

'Oh, I don't think so,' Melanie said, refusing another glass of wine with a wave of her hand. 'She's very keen to do it. She told me so.'

'But she's not got the staying-power. I hope I'm proved wrong.' For a moment they studied the subject of their conversation as she circulated amongst the guests, dispensing light-hearted chat and smiles with the ease of the experienced hostess. She met up at last with them, which was just as well as their own chat had ground to a halt. Melanie felt tense with him and she knew he was tense too. It showed in the taut muscles of his face. She was tense because she dare not allow herself to relax in his presence. But what about him? Why was he so ill at ease?

'What's the matter with you two?' Linda asked cheerfully. She was boldly made-up, diamonds flashing at throat and wrist. 'This is supposed to be fun.' She cast a mischievous glance towards

Melanie. 'What a divine dress,' she said. 'Most unexpected on you.' She laughed, holding her glass aloft. 'Sorry, I didn't mean that to sound as it did. It just seems not quite you, my dear, but it is so beautiful.'

Melanie smiled at her and then, as she disappeared, returned her gaze to Conrad. It wasn't so much tension as a wariness, she decided. Something missing. Something that had been present earlier in the afternoon was gone. She sipped the last of her drink thoughtfully, listening only half-heartedly as he began a somewhat stilted conversation about the area they were living in. She was not completely naïve. No-one could be after a relationship with Paul. Conrad was attracted to her, physically attracted, as she was to him. They both knew it and, in their different ways, were trying to deal with it. He was the sort of man who would be intensely loyal to Helen and because of that, she knew their relationship would go no further.

No matter how aware she was of him, of his strength, his magnetism, his dark good-looks, of his dreamy eyes, she had to forget him. It was depressing. But a fact.

'Penny for them?' His amused voice broke through her thoughts. 'You are not remotely interested in our average June rainfall, are you?'

'Not much. Sorry . . . I . . . ' Melanie blushed, fiddling with her small evening-bag and grateful indeed that dinner was announced at that very moment. It was quite late. There was a somewhat sedate rush to get into the dining-room.

Conrad escorted her into the softly-lit room, carefully not touching her. Outside, the sun was low in the sky, the hills settling down to slumber, their rim artificially pink and gold.

The table setting was inviting. Crystal sparkled. At each place, fluted pale-pink linen napkins, heavy-weight silver cutlery, and, holding centre stage, Melanie's flowers. She found herself sandwiched between George Richards and a defiant-looking Kate. George struck up an immediate conversation, taking up where he had left off. They were on to the family dogs by now, two boisterous retrievers. With a smile, Melanie confessed she would love to meet them. 'Oh good, you're a dog person,' George exclaimed with delight. 'Thought you were. Not usually wrong.' Melanie smiled, thought briefly of mentioning her own departed pet but decided against it. George would be altogether too sympathetic.

At her other side, Kate was already involved in flirting outrageously with a not unwilling Conrad. Melanie tried to listen to George, nibble at her starter and keep track of Kate's progress.

'We live down in the village, Miss Lawrence,' George continued, tucking into his starter with evident relish. 'Beechside. It's not far from the pub. Did you notice the pub? The White Horse.'

'I've not been down to the village yet.

I haven't had the time,' Melanie said apologetically. 'I'm going to take a wander down when I get the chance.'

'When you do, you must pay us a visit.' George wiped his mouth with his crumpled napkin. 'You can't beat country life. Dogs. Walks. Healthy exercise. City folk are so pale. No fresh air, you see.' He paused uncomfortably, realizing that he was addressing a city girl. 'Not that you don't . . . ' his voice petered out and he flushed with sudden embarrassment. 'No offence, I hope.'

'None, George.' Melanie touched his arm lightly. She found him immensely likeable, someone in whom she could happily confide. Further down the table, Ben was silent, looking towards Kate and frowning. Oblivious, Kate giggled loudly at something Conrad had said.

'Polly will be delighted to see you,' George went on. 'Anytime. Misses the children, you know. I'm kept fairly busy. I cover several of the smaller villages as well as our own. One or two of my patients live on isolated farms on the moor.' He leaned towards her. 'You can bet your bottom dollar, Melanie, that they need me when the road's virtually impassable. I'm expecting to have to call a helicopter out some day for a difficult delivery or some such thing. Bit of drama, eh? Winters can be dreadful. Black ice and snow. Drifts. Treacherous.'

Melanie eyed Conrad anxiously, but he was too busy playing up to Kate for all he was worth to have overheard. Kate was enjoying herself hugely, casting occasional triumphant glances towards Ben who had by now turned his attention to an animated Linda.

'I'm not being too familiar, am I . . . calling you Melanie,' George said, a worried frown on his face. 'Always been a bit hopeless at these social niceties. Polly keeps me right usually.'

'I'd like you to call me Melanie,' she said with a broad smile. For a doctor, he was surprisingly hesitant in some ways.

She placed her silver spoon on the dish. She was no longer hungry. He had not looked at her once since they sat down. If he had made a conscious decision to distance himself, he was certainly succeeding.

But he ought to distance himself, she told herself primly. From Kate too. What was he up to? Did he flirt with all the ladies? If he had an ounce of decency, he would remember poor Helen who was no doubt already tucked up in her spartan bed.

He was making it crystal-clear that their relationship would go no further. He was only doing exactly what she had hoped he would do.

Why, then, did she feel so miserable?

5

After a few hectic days when Melanie was obliged to act as hostess-helper to the assortment of guests, most of them departed amid much kissing and yells of laughter. Lunches on the terrace, sophisticated picnics on the lawns, extravagant dinners at various venues nearby, all these seemed to have been good for Linda. She was cheerful and relaxed and the door to the office remained firmly closed. In between bouts of pleasantries, Melanie often eyed it wistfully. She was longing to get started. There would be so much to do and it occurred to her that Linda would have to be jollied along or the book would never get started let alone finished.

Kate and Ben were the last to go. Ben was determined to corner Linda into making some commitment and Linda was stringing him happily along, being determinedly vague. Due back in London, he was making a last attempt, having a working breakfast with her which she thought was great fun and made her feel like a proper business-woman. Melanie found herself escorting a bored Kate round the estate. The morning was chill and clouds hung low in the sky.

'I hate the country,' Kate wailed, trailing around a few steps behind Melanie. 'I really don't know why people make such a fuss about it. I wouldn't care, quite frankly, if I didn't see a tree from one year to the next.'

Melanie laughed. 'Oh, come on, Kate,' she said briskly. 'You don't mean that. Don't you enjoy all this fresh air?'

'Fresh air! You can keep it. It plays havoc with my complexion. This pale, interesting look derives from staying indoors as much as possible.' She smiled at Melanie, a genuine smile. She certainly looked the part of a country girl, clad in cords and richly-patterned sweater, although her elaborate teased hairstyle spoilt the effect.

Melanie returned her smile. She was beginning to like Kate. It had taken some time. Kate was difficult, tactless and abrasive, but refreshingly honest, often saying things that others were thinking. She could not help it if she had had a more than comfortable upbringing and Melanie was quite unperturbed now by the occasional boasting. 'Give me the town any day,' Kate continued stoutly. 'I hate it here. These hills make me feel claustrophobic. Most of all, of course, I hate that swine Conrad Bailes.'

'Conrad? Why? What's he been up to?' Melanie asked, trying to keep her voice light and unconcerned.

'That's just it, darling. Nothing. Absolutely nothing.' Kate stopped dead and leaned against a convenient tree. 'I'm whacked,' she said. 'And my feet are killing me. I'm not used to walking. You don't happen to have a cigarette on you, do you?'

'I don't smoke.'

'Neither do I.' Kate laughed. 'I gave it up years ago. But when I'm really angry, I could murder one. Tell me, Melanie, do you remember dinner the first evening we were here? Did he or did he not give me the come-on? If that wasn't an invitation, I don't know what was.'

'He certainly seemed interested in you,' Melanie said quietly. 'But he is engaged. Didn't you know that?' Her mind was racing at Kate's words. She had seen her and Conrad together over the last few days. And wondered.

'Of course I know that.' Kate tugged her sweater down over her corded hips. 'To Helen, who we all know is confined to bed. A hospital bed where he definitely can't join her. The poor man must be desperate. At least that's what I figured. It was just meant to be a flirtation, darling, nothing more. It was all progressing rather too slowly for my liking so I decided to take the initiative, and what do you think he had the nerve to do?'

'What?' Melanie waited quietly, watching with some amusement Kate's comically tragic expression. 'Go on,' she prodded gently as Kate seemed momentarily stuck for words.

'Rebuffed me. Told me in no uncertain terms that there was another. This Helen woman. She must have a helluva hold on him. He was very serious, darling, and so . . . incredibly attractive. He made it perfectly plain that I did not interest him in the slightest.' Her eyes opened in their astonishment. 'I ask you, hasn't he got a colossal nerve. He might have given me a little kiss. What harm would that have done?'

'Maybe he thought that if he did that, it would lead to . . . he might not have been able to stop himself,' Melanie said sympathetically. She smiled at Kate, whose hurt expression had not wavered. 'After all you are very attractive,' she added, feeling the need to cheer Kate up somehow.

'Yes, I am, aren't I?' Kate beamed and Melanie relaxed. For once it seemed, she had chosen the right tack. 'That's it, of course,' Kate continued. 'Pity. He's like a time-bomb. All that sexual energy just under the surface, kept superbly under control.' She managed a smile. 'I don't suppose you've noticed.' She cast a sly look towards Melanie. 'You're a dark horse. Linda tells me that you're engaged. What's he like, this fella of yours? Tell me all.'

In the face of such eagerness, Melanie felt stumped for an answer. She was tempted for a moment to tell her the truth but decided against it. She owed it to Linda to tell her first and Linda might be hurt if she blabbed it out to Kate. 'He's . . . dishy,' she replied with a quick smile, using the expression with which Kate could best associate. She did not disappoint her.

'Really? What's he do? No, let me guess . . . ' She looked at Melanie intently. 'What sort of man would you go for? Someone highly powered? No. Someone in an incredibly steady, boring job. Am I right?'

Tactless again! Melanie laughed, bemused at Kate's logic in arriving at the latter conclusion. 'Not exactly,' she said, judging it was time to change the subject before it dipped to danger-point. The last thing she wanted was for Kate to guess her feelings for Conrad. Kate was the sort of person who would tell him straight. 'Come on, I'm getting cold,' she said, shivering theatrically. 'Let's go and get warm.'

'That's the first sensible suggestion all morning,' Kate said. 'Tea and toast by the fire.'

They walked quickly back to the house.

* * *

After Kate and Ben's departure, Linda was in a very good mood, brisk and business-like in a grey suit, white blouse and red-framed owl glasses. They seemed to be more for effect than a genuine optical reason.

'Sort through these,' she said, depositing fat files and scrap-books on Melanie's desk. 'They're all mixed up I'm afraid. Ben says I've to work out a basic plan first.' She giggled, her business-like pose faltering. 'He's so deadly serious. He and Kate are totally incompatible, wouldn't you say? Of course, she's just after him for his position. He's a minor aristocrat. I'm surprised she didn't tell you that, she's frightfully into things like that.' She frowned at the files. 'Can you get them into some sort of chronological order?'

'I'll try,' Melanie said, seeing it would take some time. It would seem from an initial glance that Linda never threw anything away. As well as photographs, heaps of them, there were bundles of unrelated receipts for everything from a saucepan to a mink coat. Rattled for a moment by the sheer size of the task, Melanie set to work, to clearing the top of an adjacent desk completely to give herself more working-space. She would enjoy this, she thought with relish, once she got going. Linda watched, amused, swinging the glasses lazily, her thoughts obviously half elsewhere.

'Can you really see people being remotely interested in me as a child?' she asked, a slight frown on her face. 'Ben says to cram it with detail. People love detail, he says. What do you think? My childhood, despite what the press would have you believe, was rather boring and middle-class.' She laughed as Melanie glanced up, surprised. 'Yes, I know, I was supposed to have been born into near poverty in some vague northern town and fought my way upwards with gritted teeth, relying all the while of course on my body.'

'Why didn't you put them right?' Melanie asked. 'They can't just print stuff like that if it's not true.'

'Philip said just forget it. Our friends know the truth and what did other people matter? That's just it, I'm afraid they do matter rather. What others think of you always matters, doesn't it?'

Melanie agreed with a little nod. 'Then you must start at the beginning as Ben suggests. People will be much more sympathetic to what happened later.'

Linda eyed her thoughtfully. 'You're quite right, my dear. You know the strangest thing was I almost came to believe that nonsense myself. A rags to riches existence is so romantic, isn't it? Daughter of a middle-ranking diplomat doesn't have quite the same impact, does it? Although they did disown me.' Her eyes twinkled and a smile played round her lips. 'Well, almost. I disappointed them dreadfully. I was their only child and Daddy hoped I would turn out to be the first woman astronaut or something equally praiseworthy. I wanted to be an actress and that, in their eyes, was a distinctly shady profession. My Aunt Agatha was an actress, you see, but it was rarely talked about.'

'But you became an actress?' Melanie

was beginning to realize what an eventful life Linda had led. It made her own life seem so very ordinary. Her parents had wanted her to become a secretary, a safe secure job, and that's exactly what she had become. Yet, at the time, she had not felt that she was doing what they wanted because it was what she wanted too. Her rebellion had come now, a little late, and she supposed that was what made it so shocking in her mother's eyes.

'I became a sort of actress,' Linda said dreamily, swinging her glasses and staring beyond Melanie at something in her past. 'I was not very successful. I blame my lack of success entirely on Mummy. I was very nearly born in Paris and that would have been so much more dramatic. Instead, she rushed home to London and I was born there. If I'd been born in France, I could have claimed to be . . . sort of French.' There was laughter in her voice but she sobered so suddenly that Melanie was left with a smile on her face as Linda continued. 'Thank goodness they did not live to hear the scandal when it broke. They were killed in a plane crash.'

'Oh, I'm so sorry,' Melanie murmured, the smile wiped from her face, her head bowed. There was a moment's silence and then Linda replaced her glasses and smiled. It was the signal to start work and for a while they did just that, Linda scribbling into a notebook and Melanie sorting the photographs into piles. Some, but not all, were labelled on the back with a brief description and the date. It was interesting to see how Linda had blossomed from a plainish twelve-year-old into a very pretty sixteen-year-old. She was getting somewhere at last when Linda's voice broke through the quiet.

'Is that the time? Let's have coffee. Be a dear, Melanie, and go and make some. We'll have a nice chat over coffee and then I think we'll take the afternoon off. I'm bored with this and I need to go shopping.'

'But we've only just got started,' Melanie felt bound to protest, only half-heartedly because she knew it was hopeless. She could tell from Linda's intent expression that she was already planning her afternoon.

'I've had quite enough for one day.' Linda pushed papers away. 'Why don't you go for a drive? You haven't seen much of the countryside yet. You can go up the dale. Conrad will tell you some of the places that will be worth a visit.'

Melanie went to make coffee. Jean was alone in the kitchen and showed no surprise when Melanie announced with some resignation that work was already over for the day.

'Don't you worry about it,' she said with a knowing smile. 'That's Linda all over. I know it makes you feel like you're not earning your money but it won't bother her at all. Just make the best of it.' She looked carefully at Melanie as she prepared coffee. 'Are you all right?' she asked kindly. 'You've had a worried look these last few days.

Was it that Kate?' She sniffed her contempt. 'Right madam she is. Brazen with it. One of the maids was telling me that . . . ' She flushed. 'Her bed was never slept in, the whole time she was here. I expect she was with that nice Mr Whitelay.'

'I expect so,' Melanie said, hiding a smile. 'Those things do happen, Jean.'

'Maybe, but . . . she wasn't satisfied with that, wasn't that madam, oh dear me no. She set her sights on poor Conrad and him an engaged man. Do you know Conrad had to . . . ' She broke off suddenly as the door opened and he stepped in, grinning.

'Conrad had to what?' he asked, his voice amused. 'Gossiping again, Jean? Who's been talking now?'

Jean's eyes widened innocently. 'I don't know what you're on about, Conrad,' she said with a smile. 'Melanie and me, we were just having a nice little chat. She's finished work for the day and she's thinking of having a little drive up the dale.'

143

'Is she now?' He eyed her solemnly, as, somewhat flustered, she added some biscuits to the tray. 'Fancy coming with me? I've got a couple of visits to make this afternoon so you might as well. It'll save me drawing you a complicated map. There's so many little lanes and if you take the wrong one, it can take you miles out of your way.'

Melanie glanced suspiciously at him. His blue eyes were warm, inviting. Did he expect her to agree? Was he just being polite and did he hope that she might refuse? In view of how he had snubbed Kate, she certainly did not want to risk him doing that to her. It would be in everyone's best interests if they went separately. But it was Jean who put a stop to that.

'How nice,' she said, looking from one to the other. 'Melanie will be able to have a little chat with Barbara up at Greyscar. You are due up there, aren't you, Conrad? Barbara's always glad of a little female company,' she added wryly with a smile directed at Melanie. 'Four

144

sons, a husband, a brother. No wonder she gets desperate for a chat about nothing.'

Conrad laughed. Melanie knew exactly what he was thinking. So, women talked about nothing did they? She glanced crossly at him but he was oblivious to her irritation. She was left with no choice for it would seem churlish to refuse this poor Barbara the chance of a womanly gossip. She picked up the tray and walked past him, accepting his invitation as she did so with a small smile.

★ ★ ★

The Range Rover sailed effortlessly up one of the steepest hills Melanie had ever come across. A blind summit, it was dizzily brief before they were off downwards. Conrad handled the car well and she felt perfectly safe but still peeved at the turn of events that had dragged her along this afternoon against her better judgement.

145

'I hope you realize that if it hadn't been for this Barbara, I'd have much preferred to drive myself,' she muttered ungraciously, and was irritated when he laughed.

'Seems a bit unnecessary for us to be in two cars going the same way,' he said reasonably. 'And, on your own, you'd have missed the nicest bits. In any case,' he added, not taking his eyes off the winding road ahead, 'I didn't think you minded my company that much.'

'It's not that,' she said, her mood totally blocking out the wild beauty of the sweeping views to left and right. It was threatening, dark clouds massing overhead, and the hills had a rare beauty, rippling still in sunlight but seemingly watchful for the blanket of clouds that would soon tumble in and engulf them. 'It's not that,' she repeated, mindful that she was being very unfair. 'It's just . . . oh, never mind,' she finished, her irritation stemming from the fact that he was so blissfully unaware of the reason for her depression. It was oh so easy for him. He was happily engaged, Helen was getting better, soon they would be married. How wonderful for him! But what about her? She was deeply unhappy, the break-up with Paul having a much deeper effect than she had expected. She was mixed-up, emotional. One thing was sure. She was not going to confess that, under any circumstances. If he did know about Paul, and she had no reason to suppose he did, then that was for the best. If he didn't, didn't she have an obligation to explain? Helen was a long way away and she was here close beside him and it would be so, so easy for something to happen, something that he would regret later. With a sigh, she wished she had never come along. Damn this Barbara, whoever she was. She should have left her to her male-dominated existence.

'It widens out a bit just here,' Conrad explained, easing off the accelerator. 'I'll pull over and we can stretch our legs and look at the view. It's quite spectacular.'

'You needn't bother. I can see it from here,' she snapped, instantly regretting the sharpness of her tone. This afternoon she was behaving like a child. She stole a glance at him as he pulled the car onto a natural lay-by. Was there the faintest hint of amusement there?

'You could see it if you were bothering to look,' he remarked. 'You're too busy being annoyed with me and I don't know why.'

He was perfectly right, but how could she explain that if she ceased to be angry, she might very well burst into tears. She had to be on guard the whole time. She did not want a repetition of the Kate incident, so she was trying very very hard to ignore the wild racing of her pulse whenever she caught his gaze.

'Are we going to get out or are you going to sit here and sulk?' he said with a teasing smile on his face as the silence lengthened.

'We might as well get out now that we've stopped,' Melanie said, struggling ridiculously with her door as it refused to open.

'Allow me.' He was trying not to laugh. He leaned across and was suddenly very close, too close. She could hear his breathing, see the beginning of bristle on his chin, smell his clean male scent. His arm brushed against her softly. If she did not know better, she would have said quite deliberately. Somewhat shakily, she climbed out. The clouds were thudding on, patches of blue rapidly disappearing. It was cool and quiet. She leaned against the stone wall and shivered.

'Cold? Do you want a jacket? There's one in the back somewhere.'

'No . . . no thanks.' She kept her face averted so that he could not see her eyes, which she knew would be luminous from the threat of tears.

'See that hill over there,' he said, pointing out a peak so perfect it looked unreal, a child's vision of what a hill should be. 'I've been up there. It's not as high as it looks. A day's climb, a gentle sort of climb, nothing too strenuous. Anyone could do it.'

'Even me?' She had found her voice but it sounded strange and forced.

'Even you.' It was a quiet response, low and husky. How she loved his voice. And his smile. And his eyes. Everything about him.

'How's Helen these days?' she asked, confident now that she could control the promise of tears. She had to keep reminding him about Helen. Had to. For both their sakes.

'I saw her yesterday.' He burrowed deeper into the chunkiness of his sweater. 'Physically she's improving all the time, but mentally . . . well, let's say she's changed. She's distant. She wouldn't even talk about the wedding and usually that cheers her up.' He smiled a little. 'It'll be different once she's out of there.'

'Of course it will,' Melanie said brightly. 'You'll have to be patient with her. She's been through a lot.'

'Perhaps she worries that I might leave her . . . ' He paused. 'I won't. I'll stand by her, you know.' He glanced at her with a little smile. 'Melanie, I haven't told . . . ' He stopped very suddenly and stared unseeingly ahead.

Melanie eyed him curiously. What had he been about to say? She shivered, very chill, and he took the hint and ushered her back into the car. Melanie brooded a little on his words. He was quite determined to let her know that he wouldn't leave Helen. Who was he trying to convince? Her or himself?

It was late afternoon when they arrived at Greyscar and the bumpy track that led down to the farm. The smell of the farmyard was still a surprise to someone who had breathed town all her life. Barbara was there to greet them holding a plump, unsmiling baby in her arms, a toddler clinging to her leg. She called out cheerfully to Conrad, 'Hello there,' smiling as she was introduced to Melanie. 'Come on inside,' she said. 'The men will have business to discuss.'

Bemused, Melanie followed her. The kitchen was a huge room, warm, with a table spread with colouring-books, pencils and a half-done jigsaw. Melanie apologized for intruding, noticing the pile of ironing and the preparations for a meal. 'Would you like me to help?' she offered with a smile, hoping Barbara wouldn't take her up on it. Her culinary skills were below par, she reflected. It was high time she stopped merely reading cookery books and had a go at the practicalities.

'It can wait. I'm glad of an excuse to stop,' Barbara said decisively. She put the baby down to sleep and the older children took the toddler in tow. For the moment they had time to themselves and Barbara breathed a sigh of relief. She looked curiously at Melanie. She had large, most attractive blue eyes and long, model-like lashes.

'He has told you he's engaged, hasn't he?' she asked, smiling and indicating a

152

batch of freshly baked scones. 'Do help yourself.'

'Thank you. They look delicious.' She considered Barbara's question. 'Oh yes, I know he's engaged to Helen. We're just friends,' she added hastily. 'Colleagues. We both happen to work for Linda.'

Barbara looked at her thoughtfully. 'Oh good, for a minute I wondered if he had told you. It was just the way I caught him looking at you ... for a moment I ... ' There was a surprising trace of a blush on her face. 'I don't suppose you've met Helen. Quiet girl. Difficult to get to know. I never quite felt that she and Conrad ... ' She stopped. 'Are you helping Mrs Fletcher-Grant with her book?' she asked, changing the subject deftly, and not before time Melanie felt with some amusement.

The time passed pleasantly enough; photographs of the children were produced and the conversation veered from pure trivia to politics. Barbara proved to be an intelligent, capable woman and Melanie liked her. She saw little of life outside the dale but it didn't seem to matter to her too much. When Conrad returned, they made their goodbyes, Melanie careful not to stray too close to him whilst Barbara was there, watchful.

'How did you get on with Barbara?' Conrad asked as they drove on through a light drizzle.

'Very well. I don't envy her, though. She must get lonely.'

'Lonely? With all those children?'

'You know exactly what I mean.' She stared out at the fine rain and the steadily darkening landscape. 'It's getting late,' she said, noticing that they were not heading back. 'Have you another call to make?'

'No. I'm taking you out to dinner,' he said with a quick smile. 'One of my favourite pubs. It's very popular round here. I managed to book a table when we were at the farm. They can just squeeze us in.'

'You might have asked,' Melanie protested faintly. 'I'm hardly dressed for dinner.'

'Why not? You look fine.'

'Yes, but . . . ' She stopped. There was no point in going on about it. She should say no and have done with it. She should insist he drive her back to Headmoor at once. And yet, what would be the harm in it? They were tired. The air had seemed extra fresh at the farm, which was on very high ground. Somehow tiring. She had found herself yawning a short while ago. Dinner out would be rather nice. She could ask him about America, about his business venture there. It needn't be a soft lights, sweet music, holding hands sort of dinner. She murmured her acceptance with a sinking heart. Oh why was Helen in hospital? Somehow it made it all so sordid. Sneaky and behind her back. Was she really trying to steal him away from Helen? And if so, she ought to be ashamed. It was a terrible thing to

155

contemplate doing. She realized she was twisting her hands anxiously and calmed herself. Stop it.

'You're very quiet.' He switched on the head-lamps. 'It's going to get dark very early tonight,' he remarked casually, glancing at her. 'Are you all right?'

'Have you taken Helen to this place?' The question was out before she could help it.

'So that's it.' He chuckled. 'Don't worry. I'll tell her all about it. She's very understanding.'

'Yes, she is,' Melanie said drily.

'She trusts me,' he snapped, stilling her by his tone. 'Like your bloke trusts you. Can't we just have a pleasant meal together?'

So, he knew about Paul. It was no secret and no doubt Linda had told him. What must he really think of her? If she had still been engaged to Paul would she have agreed to go out for a meal with another man? Of course not. She sank into a silence that lasted until they reached the pub, a brightly lit low-slung building with a small, crowded car park. They followed another couple into the glowing interior, the girl wearing a velvet skirt and satin blouse. Melanie smoothed down her cotton skirt and felt distinctly under-dressed.

'I thought you said they didn't dress up,' she hissed as they waited in the beamed entrance.

'Did I say that?' He smiled at her, his eyes travelling the length and breadth of her in a single slow movement. 'You look lovely,' he said. 'I don't know what you're getting so worked up about?'

A man whom she assumed to be the proprietor came to greet them. Obviously he knew Conrad and a slight hesitation in his manner as he turned to look at her was deftly put aside. No questions. But Melanie knew at once that Helen had been here with him and guilt rose in her as they were led through the main dining-room into a small side-room. 'This all right for you, sir?' The manager's voice was apologetic. 'We've a silver wedding through there and so we're a little full tonight.'

'This will be fine,' Conrad assured him with a smile. There was just one other table already occupied by another couple with whom they exchanged a polite smile. Melanie was all too aware of her casual dress and sank down thankfully, trying to hide herself against the wall and behind the huge menu.

She was startled when Conrad tugged at it, laughing into her face. 'If you're worried about your dress, forget it. You're easily the most beautiful girl here. That's why they were looking at you as you came through.'

His voice was a mere whisper and her heart hammered at the words. Carefully, she looked down at the pale blue of the tablecloth, her voice a whisper too, but dangerously so. 'Please don't say things like that,' she said. 'Let's keep this strictly on a business level, shall we? There's lots to talk about. You can tell me all about this business idea of yours for a start.'

He raised his eyebrows, quite unrepentant. 'Do you really want to know? Then you shall. After we've ordered,' he added as the waitress appeared. For a moment, after she left them, they were silent and it was impossible not to listen in to what was being said at the other table. The woman had a ringing voice as well as alarmingly large earrings and was conducting her private conversation as if she was addressing an eager audience.

'So, Colin, I told her straight. I said she'll have to go. I expect reliability and it's no use whatsoever if I can't be sure that she'll be there on time to pick Jackie up. I will not have my daughter waiting at school for her to deign to turn up.'

'Quite right, dear. Is your steak all right?'

Conrad gave a little polite cough and guiltily Melanie returned her attention to him. 'Lake Champlain stretches right up into Canada,' he began with a smile.

'No, it's not a travel lecture, I'm just putting vou in the picture. Have you heard of it?'

'Vaguely,' Melanie confessed. 'It sounds beautiful, but then I love lakes.'

'There's nothing on our side of the lake for miles,' he went on. 'It's crying out for a motel. There'll be views over the lake and it's near a ferry crossing into New York State. Ideal site. Perfect for people touring New England, going up maybe into Canada or going across into New York State and the Champlain valley. Remote and yet not too far from civilization.' He gave a distant smile, memory in his eyes. 'We thought we'd have an English theme. The restaurant will be an olde-worlde inn, a bit like this, but we'll have the waitresses dressed up as serving-wenches. And the menu will be full of medieval-sounding dishes. It should go down a bomb. What do you think?'

'I'm not sure,' Melanie said, thinking about it. 'Isn't it just a touch corny if you don't mind me saying so?'

He laughed. 'Let me explain . . . ' He paused as their starter arrived and, at the next table, the one-sided conversation continued.

'After all, Colin, au pairs are supposed to be learning the language, aren't they? She makes no effort. None at all. I have to struggle along with my French and it's all such an effort. And a bore.'

'She jolly well ought to learn.'

Melanie and Conrad exchanged a smile. 'Americans like corn,' he said earnestly. 'They go for things like that. Don't get me wrong, they're great people. It'll be something different. They get a bit sick of club sandwiches and hash browns and muffins.'

'All right,' Melanie said ruefully. 'I take your point.' She smiled up at the proprietor as he appeared briefly to enquire if everything was to madam's satisfaction. Everything was.

The sweet-trolley had arrived at the next table. The couple had selected from it and were still debating the fate of the au pair.

'It worries me that people will think we're not doing our bit for the European Community,' the man said. 'If we send her back, how's that going to look?'

'What's more important, Colin, the welfare of your child or the piffling European Community?'

She got shushed for that remark and Melanie hid a smile. 'What does Helen think about your plans?' she asked. She had almost forgotten Helen and had forced herself to ask the question. Conrad's face clouded.

'That's just it,' he said. 'She doesn't want to go. She wants me to back out of it. There's still time for me to do that. It won't upset things too much if I do, but . . . damn it, I want to give it a try.' He reached for his napkin. 'Look, I thought we'd agreed that this was our meal. Just you and me. Don't let's spoil it.'

Spoil it? By talking about his fiancée? They continued their meal and it was indeed easy to forget her. After leisurely coffee and mints, they stepped outside into darkness. The moon was nearly full and the clouds had passed by, allowing a million stars to twinkle their pulsing beats. This time Melanie was grateful for the jacket he found her and she slipped it round her shoulders as they began the long drive back.

She was full of chat. About her old job at Johnson's. About her town. About her father. A brief mention of her mother. Nothing about Paul. He listened. It was a pleasant, animated drive and Melanie was sorry as she realized they were turning into the gates of Headmoor at last.

'Thank you,' she said simply when he had parked the car and was escorting her to the door. 'It's been lovely. I've enjoyed it.'

Their footsteps were loud on the drive. The house was in darkness, moonlight showing them their way, casting shadows over the lawns. There was the scent of flowers in the air as they walked past the wide herbaceous border. Conrad laughed, stopping below the pendulous branches of a weeping tree. 'One thing is worrying me,' he said. 'It's been on my mind all the way back. In fact, I think I may well lose sleep over it.'

'What?' Melanie looked at him, puzzled. She tugged the jacket a little closer.

'Should they or should they not get rid of that damned au pair?' he asked with a grin.

Melanie's laughter was immediate and she smiled up at him as his laughter rang out too. 'That's better,' he said. 'I like to hear you laugh.' He caught her arm and pulled her towards him. There was stillness all around. No sound. As if everything was holding its breath. Waiting for this moment. She heard his breathing, ragged. He traced a finger down her face whilst she looked on in astonishment. She should ask what did he think he was doing. She should remind him about Helen.

Quickly. Instead, she said nothing, marvelling at the feathery touch of his finger caressing her face, lingering over her lips, moving down to her throat.

'What's he like, this bloke of yours?' he asked roughly. 'What sort of man would let me do this to you? And this?' He was kissing her now, little exasperating kisses, fleeting touches, all over her face and throat. 'And this?' He paused to stare at her, his eyes dreamy. 'You're so beautiful, my sweetheart,' he whispered and at last kissed her properly.

She gave up all pretence. What did Helen matter? The jacket slipped from her as he pressed his hands onto her back, drawing her near. She slid her arms up and around him, touching the hair at his nape, holding him, drowning in the sweetness of the lingering kiss. 'Oh, Conrad,' she whispered when he moved his lips away with a sigh.

He disentangled her arms and pushed her away, a touch roughly. 'So your bloke trusts you, does he?' he said, hurt in his voice. 'And Helen trusts me, dammit. We ought to be ashamed of ourselves for doing that.'

'No . . . no . . . ' Melanie tried to draw him back to her. His body was suddenly tight, unyielding. Miserably, she reeled away. 'Paul . . . ' she began. 'My fiancé, that is . . . he . . . '

What was the matter with her? Why didn't she just come straight out with it? It was already too late. The sweetness of the moment had gone and his mouth was set in a firm line. 'We mustn't see each other again,' he said. 'Not alone like this. It's my fault. I thought I could handle it, but I can't. I should never have asked you out to dinner.' Despair flitted over his face and he turned away. 'You should never have come to dinner. You looked so beautiful. I felt proud. For a time back there, I almost forgot Helen.'

'You still love her?' The question hurt but she had to know.

He did not answer, merely picked up the jacket that still lay on the ground and strode away. Slowly, she walked up to her room. By the time she reached it, she was weeping. Great sobs escaped from her as she closed the door and flung herself on the bed. It had been so wonderful. She had wanted him to go on kissing her again and again and never stop. But he had stopped. For Helen.

'Damn Helen!' she cried aloud through her tears. She lay fully clothed on top of the bed, her hair a splash of colour on the white pillow, her face damp and streaked with the remains of make-up.

At last, she slept.

6

She awoke, stiff, cold and unrefreshed, remembering at once. She lay still a moment, then stretched like a kitten, basking in the memory of his kisses, his touch. Feather-light. Thrilling. Then she came back to earth with a bump. It was over. Because of Helen, because of his loyalty to Helen. Misplaced loyalty, surely, for he could not kiss her like that and not mean it. His kisses had held a sweetness she had not experienced before, and a promise. A promise of so much.

The ringing of the telephone in her sitting-room roused her fully. With a groan, she went to answer it. It was Linda, sounding altogether too bright and breezy for Melanie's sombre mood. She came straight to the point. 'I've got to go out today,' she said. 'A duty visit to Newcastle to see Helen. I'm sure you can find something to do whilst I'm gone.' There was a short silence whilst Melanie struggled to find something to say. 'Are you all right?' Linda continued, concern in her voice. 'I didn't wake you, did I? I suppose you were awfully late last night. Where did you get to? We nearly sent a search-party out.' She waited for Melanie to join in her laugh. 'Before you say anything about the work, there's plenty of time for that. I refuse to be rushed. We'll make an early start tomorrow and work our heads off.'

'Did you say you were going to see Helen?' Melanie at last managed to croak. 'I thought you hated hospitals.'

'I do. You wouldn't like to come with me, would you? You could give me a bit of moral support. I may need it. She's summoned me, actually. She's written to ask me to go to see her. It all sounds very mysterious. There's something she wants to tell me, she says.'

Melanie's heart turned a slow somersault. 'What?' she asked.

'I don't know yet, do I?' Linda gave a trill of laughter. 'She told me not to tell anyone, so mum's the word. She especially told me not to tell Conrad, so the mystery deepens. Those two haven't been having words, have they?'

Melanie clutched the receiver tightly. 'Not that I know of,' she said quietly.

'Where *did* he take you last night?' The question was casually put but Melanie was quick to detect the hidden meaning behind it.

'Up the dale to Greyscar,' she said defensively. 'And then it was getting late and we stopped off for dinner.'

'Did you now?' Linda's voice had cooled imperceptibly but, heightened as Melanie's senses were, she recognized it and felt a desperate need to explain.

'It was perfectly innocent . . . ' she began, regretting she had even bothered to try. 'Just a friendly dinner, that's all.'

'You needn't make excuses, Melanie,' Linda said briskly. 'I shan't mention it to Helen just in case she takes it the wrong way.'

Melanie sighed as she replaced the receiver. She fingered a long length of her tangled hair. What must Linda think of her?

She caught sight of herself in the mirror. She looked terrible. Tear-stained face. Crumpled clothes. Life could not stop because of this thing with Conrad. She had to forget him. He was going soon so that would make it easier. Quickly, she stripped off her clothes and stepped into the shower, where the warm jets of water soon soothed her. Lazily she soaped herself and held her face up to the spray and washed the tears away.

She began to feel a little better as she dressed. A softly gathered skirt and blouse. She would work all day on Linda's book, on the preparations, she decided, as she crossed the hall. There was no sign of Conrad and for that she was thankful. She must try to avoid him for the next few days to give it time to settle, for the hurt to dissolve, for sanity to return.

She made coffee and toast and carried it through to the office, avoiding Jean also as she had no wish to become involved in an interrogation, no matter how gentle. She knew Jean was fond of Conrad and was aware that Jean would not approve of her stepping between him and Helen.

Resolute, she set to work, becoming so absorbed in what she was doing that it was well past lunchtime before she realized it. She stretched and pushed the papers aside. Content with her morning's efforts. Things were beginning to take shape. Linda's early life was clicking neatly into place. Somewhat furtively, not wanting to meet up with Jean, she crept into the kitchen to make herself a light snack which she carried into the conservatory.

It was already very warm, the sun having made an early start too. She sank onto one of the comfortable chairs and cast her eyes on the tranquil lawns without. The sounds and sights of nature were so comforting, but today of all days she was hard put to find solace in them.

'What are you doing here?'

She looked up in surprise. Conrad was standing in the doorway, wearing jeans and an open-necked cotton shirt. Heart thudding, she took immediate refuge in annoyance. 'I'm allowed to be here, aren't I?' she said briskly. 'I'm having a late lunch, as you can see. Linda's gone out so the day's my own.' She held the plate towards him. 'Fancy a cheese and pickle sandwich?'

He shook his head and, uninvited, sat down beside her, uncomfortably close. Ridiculously she tried to edge away. 'Where's she gone?' he asked, stretching out his long legs.

'I've no idea. Shopping, I think,' she said lightly. 'She didn't say where.'

He laughed. 'You have an impossibly innocent face,' he said. 'You can't lie convincingly, my sweetheart.'

She knew she had blushed and was irritated. Why couldn't she behave like a sane, sophisticated woman? 'Don't call me your sweetheart,' she said helplessly. 'You promised.'

'Promised what?' With a moan, he caught her hand and pulled her to her feet.

Boldly, he was now looking at her, willing her to look at him. 'I know what I said last night, but Helen needn't know and you're . . . you're so lovely. Come here . . . I need you close to me.'

'No,' she murmured, meaning yes. 'Please don't make me, Conrad.'

'I won't *make* you do anything. Don't fight it. We both want it, don't we?' He was drawing her closer and her resistance, never on a very firm footing, was weakening fast. Helen need never know, and she wanted him so much that nothing else mattered. A few fleeting moments, if that was all they could ever have . . . then, so be it. He reached out and touched her hair, running his fingers through it, smelling its newly-washed smell, rubbing at her neck, tracing his finger deliciously down the cleavage of her blouse, breathing more heavily, his blue eyes hazy now with desire.

'Please . . . ' She didn't want this to happen. Yet she did want this to happen. She should pull away now before it was too late. A few more minutes and she would be completely lost. Lost in him. No, it was already too late, she realized, as a low sound of longing escaped her throat as, with tears in her eyes, she surrendered to his searching lips. Exploring the taste of him. Loving him. She closed her eyes, smiling as he fumbled with the buttons of her blouse, releasing it at last and slipping it softly off her shoulders. She still smiled as she heard his intake of breath at her near nakedness under the flimsy bra.

Dreamily she opened her eyes then and looked at him. He called her name, his voice thick with longing. Slowly and sensuously, watching her the whole time, he touched her aching breasts. A tiny smile playing round his lips, he lowered his lips to kiss them.

Fascinated, Melanie watched as he unhooked the front-fastening clasp and began to stroke her breasts, freed now from the confines of the satiny web.

'No ... not here,' she gasped, stopping the movement of his hand with hers. Common sense surfaced reluctantly. 'It's too ... ' She laughed shakily. 'Anyone can see. Anyone could walk in.'

'Then where?' He had pulled away, breathing hard, fighting for control.

'My room,' she said, recovering her blouse and fastening it with trembling fingers. She was flushed and heady. The ache was travelling all through her veins, her nerve-endings were on full alert, expecting his touch, wanting his touch, needing his touch. She realized she wanted him to kiss her everywhere and blushed afresh at the thought. And Paul had called her cold! 'I'll go up,' she whispered, running a hand through her tousled hair.

'I'll follow you,' he said, his smile as

shaky as hers. 'Give me ten minutes, my sweetheart.'

They laughed at that. 'Make sure it is,' she said lightly, peeping out to check if anyone was about. No-one was. She felt she must look at this moment so transparently in love that it would be obvious to anyone who saw her. And she could not trust herself to speak, not feeling so vibrantly alive and anticipatory as she did.

Once in her room, she brushed her teeth, brushed her hair. Cleaned the make-up off her face. She looked at herself and marvelled afresh at the glow love had given her.

She slipped into a silky yellow and white robe. Underneath she wore nothing, her body damp from a dizzyingly brief shower. She waited for him.

★ ★ ★

There he was! She had left the door slightly ajar for him and heard it close softly behind him. Barefoot, she padded through to meet him. 'Conrad, I . . . ' Her voice tailed away as she saw the man lounging against the door.

Paul smiled at her. 'Well, well,' he said. 'Expecting someone?'

'What are you doing here?' She could barely get the words out in sudden anxiety. 'How did you get in? And how did you know where I was?'

'Questions, questions . . . ' He was affecting a bored voice, slumping down unasked on the sofa. 'Does it matter how I found you? You didn't really expect me to leave it at that, did you? As I said, people who cross me have to suffer for it. I was just biding my time, that's all. I knew that sooner or later there would be something I could do to get back at you.'

'Stop being childish, Paul. That's . . . ridiculous,' she said, trying to keep her voice light, trying to hide the sudden panic that had gripped her like a vice. Had that been a tap just now at the door? She looked helplessly towards it. Paul had heard it too.

'Better answer it,' he said with a curt nod. 'That'll be lover-boy no doubt.'

Pulling her robe tightly around her, she opened the door. Conrad stood there, his expression changing as he caught sight of Paul lounging on the sofa.

'Conrad, I . . . ' Melanie gestured towards Paul. 'I'm sorry . . . '

'Come and join us, Conrad,' Paul called in a cheerful voice. 'I've just arrived. Paying a surprise visit to my fiancée. Come and have a celebratory drink with us.'

'No thanks . . . ' Conrad glanced briefly at her, the light fading from his eyes. 'I'll leave you alone . . . ' He exchanged a tortured glance with Melanie before turning away.

'I hope you're satisfied,' Melanie said icily as she closed the door behind him. 'And I'd like to remind you that I am not your fiancée.' She bit her lip at the prospect of all the explaining she would have to do. 'Will you excuse me . . . '

179

she said, vehemently polite. 'I'd like to get changed.'

'Into something uncomfortable?' He grinned at her. 'Stay as you are, Melanie. I like the way that thing moulds itself round you.' He reached into his pocket and pulled out his cigarette-case. 'Mind if I smoke?' He was already lighting his cigarette, watching her through half-closed eyes. Melanie's panic had receded just a little and she was desperately thinking how she should deal with this situation. She was beginning to realize what a dangerous man he was. Her leaving him had hit at his very core. 'Why didn't you tell me you were coming to work for Linda Fletcher-Grant?' he asked, exhaling blue smoke towards the ceiling.

'Isn't it obvious?' Melanie said tartly. 'I knew you'd cause trouble if you knew. How *did* you find out?'

'Does it matter? Sources, my love, sources. I intend to get an interview. An exclusive. She has an interested following has our Linda, readers who like to follow her every move. People like her get up their noses, you see, and they like to see her come a cropper.' He looked impatiently at Melanie who had, unknowingly, begun to pace the room. 'Sit down for God's sake. Is it true she had a party recently? A bit off, that, don't you think? How long ago is it since he kicked the bucket? Was a certain hairdresser at the party? And if not, why not? We have a lot of questions to ask, Melanie.'

'We?' She picked up on that. 'I'm not asking any questions.'

'But we wheedled you into this job so that we could get a behind-the-scenes angle on it, didn't we?'

'What?'

'You heard. It's not going to look too good for you, is it? She's not going to like it.' He was walking towards her, slowly. 'You look very desirable,' he said. 'Little Miss Prim suddenly looks desirable. But not for me . . . '

She had backed away as far as she

could. She was hemmed against the wall. 'I don't want you to kiss me, Paul,' she said. 'Please don't try.'

'Whatever makes you think I would want to?' His face was close up against hers. He touched the thin garment covering her. 'What happened to Miss Prim? Wait until we're married indeed!'

'I . . . I love Conrad,' she said, wriggling out of his grasp. 'Touch me once more and I'll scream.'

He raised his hands in mock surrender. 'What dramatics! I have no intention of touching you. Conrad's welcome to you.'

'Paul . . . I wish you hadn't taken this so badly. We could have stayed friends if nothing else.'

'Not a chance, darling.' He moved away. 'I'm going. I'll see Mrs Fletcher-Grant, our Linda, when she gets back.'

'If you say anything, I shall deny it.'

'My word against yours then.' He smiled. 'I wonder who she will believe?'

She was still astonished at the extent

of his hate. 'You'd get me the sack?' she asked softly.

'You humiliated me, Melanie, and nobody does that,' he said, reaching over and stubbing out his cigarette on a pretty pot ash-tray. The finality of the movement hit her squarely. Silently she watched him go.

* * *

Where was Conrad now? She had to find him, to explain. She flew back into the bedroom and whipped off the robe, stepping briskly into her clothes. She was just about to leave when the telephone jangled. She let it ring a moment, hesitating, almost closing the door on it. Office procedure drummed into her as it was, she could not do it.

'Yes,' she said abruptly into it.

'Linda here.' The line was bad. 'I'm on my way home. I'll be about an hour. I'm utterly exhausted. I've had a foul day. What have you been doing?'

'Working. This morning,' she amended guiltily. 'I got through quite a lot. We can start to sieve through it and pick out what you consider relevant.'

'Oh, marvellous!' Linda said, not very enthusiastically. 'Next time Ben threatens me with deadlines, I shall say we are working flat out.' There was a pause and Melanie could sense the agitation. 'Helen was in such a state. She quite overwhelmed me. She must have been saving up the tears for months and they erupted on me. She's calmed down now, but . . . '

'What's she so upset about?' Melanie asked, a knot of despair beginning to form within her.

'She's broken off the engagement.'

'She's done . . . what?'

'Isn't it frightful news? She wants me to tell him. Or, if I can't face that, I have a letter from her to give to him.'

'Oh, Linda, that's not fair, expecting you to do that.' Melanie was dazed, uncertain.

'That's exactly what I told her but

she was adamant. She refuses to see him again. She wants to make a clean break of it.'

Surely this should make things so much simpler. They were free now to pursue their own relationship, Melanie told herself, her mind spinning as she tried to concentrate on what Linda was saying. Why then, did she still feel an ice-cold knot inside? What was Linda saying? She struggled to listen.

'This line is quite dreadful, Melanie. I really will have to ring off . . . '

'Linda . . . wait . . . ' But it was too late. The line was dead. And she had not even broached the delicate subject of Paul. Would he go ahead with his threat? Yes, she felt sure he would. Did Linda know her well enough to laugh it off? Or would she, too, be taken in by his charm? She was easily swayed by an attractive man, she had shown that with the plausible Christofer-Jon, so it was highly likely she would.

She set out to find Conrad. She could not forget the hurt on his face when he had looked beyond her and seen Paul. What a mess! She ran across the lawns towards the river and sure enough he was there, alone, beside the stepping-stones. Silent and still. Melanie stopped, panting with the effort, the sounds of her footsteps silenced too. 'Conrad!' she called, her voice awkward and strangled. When he gave no response, she edged forward, dropping onto her knees at his side and touching his shoulders. Gently she lowered her head. 'Conrad, darling,' she whispered. 'I had no idea Paul was coming. I wouldn't have had that happen for the world.'

'Wouldn't you?' The hurt was everywhere, in his very being. 'How do you think I felt at that moment? If I could have crept into a hole, I would have. There I was just about to make love to you ... steal you away from him ... and there he was. Looked a nice bloke too ... '

'It's over between me and Paul,' she said quietly. 'It was over before I came to work here but I didn't want to upset Linda by telling her that.' She realized she was absent-mindedly kneading his shoulders, the muscles tense below her restless fingers.

'Is that true?' He turned to look at her, hope in his eyes. 'You don't love him?'

She shook her head. 'I love you,' she said softly. 'As if you didn't know that already.'

'And I love you, my sweet. If only . . . ' He turned away. 'I won't let Helen down. I'm going to go through with this for her sake. We'll just have to . . . '

'Helen's broken off your engagement,' Melanie interrupted, smiling at him. 'I shouldn't really be telling you this but . . . it's for the best, isn't it? Sympathy isn't a very strong basis for marriage, is it?'

He stiffened. Startled, she removed her hands as if his shoulders were hot coals, because she sensed he resented her touch. 'What the hell have you been saying to her?' he said sharply. 'Helen would never break off our engagement without some cause . . . ' He stared at her, a coldness descending on him. 'You told her, didn't you? You must have really upset her to make her do that. How could you?'

'I told her nothing.' She got to her feet. 'I don't know what you're making such a fuss about. It has nothing to do with me. Her decision has nothing to do with me. She doesn't even know me. It's your own guilt, Conrad, that you've got to come to terms with. If you love me . . . ' She choked on the words. 'If you love me, then I just don't understand.'

He ran a hand wearily through his hair. 'I can do without all this,' he said as if to himself. 'I've had a letter from my pal in the States. He wants an answer.'

'Then hadn't you better go,' Melanie said quietly. 'It's obviously what you want to do. I don't see what you're dithering about quite frankly. And now that Helen's . . . ' She paused, unwilling to say it. 'Well, she didn't want to go, did she? So now there's nothing to stop you, is there?'

He said nothing. He picked up a pebble and threw it into the stream. She watched the ripples. Then walked away.

7

She would have slept late next morning had it not been for a tapping on her door. Drowsily, she stumbled out of bed, wrapped a towelling gown round her, and padded to the door. If that was Conrad, thinking he could apologize for yesterday, he'd better think again! She would let him sweat a while before she condescended to accept his apology. What a lot of fuss about nothing! Accusing her of blabbing all to Helen. As if she would. The idea was preposterous.

It was Jean, armed with a breakfast-tray and a smile.

'Breakfast in bed?' Melanie managed a smile. 'Come on in, Jean, what's brought this on? I'm not usually so honoured.'

'I wanted a talk, love.' Jean set about pouring the tea. 'Linda's upset. That young man of yours has been to see her. I don't know what went on but I showed him in. Luckily, Linda was up as it happened, although she was in her negligée. Not that she didn't look very proper,' she added with a little smile.

'Paul's been to see her?' Melanie sank down onto the sofa, clutching her cup. 'Oh no. He did threaten to, but I had hoped that perhaps he would change his mind . . . ' She shook her head blindly. 'Oh, Jean, why is life so cruel? Everybody else can break off an engagement and that's the end of it, but not me . . . I have to get landed with someone who's determined to have his revenge.'

'Good job you didn't marry him,' Jean said calmly. 'Some men can keep their nasty moods quiet until after the wedding and then . . . ' Her eyes were sad. There was a ring on her finger and for a moment Melanie wondered what her husband had been like. Now was not the moment to probe.

'I've been having a little chat with

Conrad,' Jean continued, helping herself to buttered toast. 'Poor man! He's taken it hard, this break-up with Helen. They were never right for each other,' she added firmly. 'I knew. Call me a romantic, maybe, but I can always tell. When two people are right, then . . . '

'You're as bad as my father,' Melanie said with a laugh. 'He's a romantic too.'

'Is there a chance of you and Conrad . . . are you going with him, love?'

Melanie turned her face away, feeling tears threaten. 'He hasn't asked me,' she said. 'Or at least . . . ' She paused, remembering. 'He did once ask if I'd be prepared to move to America and I said something silly like it was an awful long way away. And he said . . . ' She stopped. 'If he asked me now, I'd say yes.'

'He's stubborn,' Jean said. 'Got himself in a tizzy about Helen. Blamed himself for the accident and hasn't stopped blaming himself ever since. He was going to marry her when . . . well, he told me some time ago that his feelings had changed. He told me that . . . ' She smiled. 'I don't need to tell you, do I? I hope things work out for you.'

'Thank you, Jean.' Melanie stood up, running her hands through her hair. 'I'd better go down, I suppose.'

'You'd better.' Jean was suddenly brisk, tidying the tray. 'Didn't I tell you? Linda wants to see you.'

She dressed in record time, feeling like a condemned man. Jean had said Linda was upset. Upset but not angry? Had she seen through Paul? She forced herself to stop worrying about it. There was no point until she had seen Linda. If Paul had won her over then it was already much too late.

* * *

'I'll be brief,' Linda said. She was dressed in a pale sorbet pink and her voice was icy to match. Her whole being was stiff and unyielding. Melanie remained standing as she had not been asked to sit. 'There's very little to say,' she said. 'Except that I want you to leave. As soon as possible.'

'Oh, Linda . . . please let . . . '

Linda held up her hand. 'No. I don't want to listen to you begging. That really is unnecessary. I thought I could trust you and I see now that you've been lying to me all along. You got this job under false pretences, didn't you, a little accomplice for this man of yours?'

'That's not true,' Melanie said quickly. 'It's over between Paul and me. It was over long since.' She took a deep breath. 'I know I told you otherwise but I did it with the best of intentions. I just didn't want to upset you with my problems. You were coping so well, it seemed unfair. Believe me . . . '

'Spare me, Melanie.' The frostiness had not thawed. 'Did it not occur to you that if you had told me the truth, that Paul was a reporter . . . that I would not have given you the job?'

'Of course it did,' Melanie said

miserably. 'That's why I didn't tell you. I didn't tell him I was coming to work for you. I don't know how he's found out, but he's devious. And vindictive,' she added harshly. 'How I could ever have imagined myself in love with him . . . I must have shut my eyes to the way he really was.'

To her surprise Linda laughed, playing with the flowing crêpe belt on her dress. 'I thought him utterly charming. A most attractive man. He said you'd say precisely what you have just said. People who've deceived me always expect me to turn round and forgive.' Her face was pale, the pale pink of her lipstick giving her a ghost-like aura. 'I will discuss it no further. Please leave.'

There was nothing more to say. Just as she turned to go, Linda's voice rang out. 'And Conrad's going too . . . ' she said. 'He's flying out to Boston in a few days, so I really am left in the lurch.'

The words echoing in her mind, Melanie hurried upstairs, throwing things into her suitcases. She had to get out of the house before she met up again with Linda. Jean had been so kind but there wasn't even time to say goodbye to her. She had to go. Now. This very minute.

It was only as she drove out of the gates that it occurred to her that she did not know where she was going. She pulled over and leaned against the steering-wheel. Think, Melanie, think. Of course she could go home. Her father had said in one of his recent phone calls that she was welcome anytime. Her mother was coming round. Slowly. But she could not possibly go home yet, not with so much unresolved. She certainly had no intention of confronting Paul. Let him do what he liked. She never wanted to see him again.

What should she do then? She could hardly afford the luxury of an hotel, not for more than a few days at least, and she didn't know how long she would be staying. In all honesty, what was the point of staying? Linda had dismissed her. Conrad was off in a few days to the States. What was the point indeed? Yet she could not bring herself to give up on them. Not yet. Linda had once said that it mattered what people thought of you. She was right. It mattered very much.

Drumming her fingers on the wheel, the solution reared up. Of course! George and Polly! They had said they would be happy to see her anytime and she was sure they had meant it. Surely they would not turn her away, even if they were friends of Linda too.

Not quite sure what to expect and dreading a rebuff, she drove into the village, finding their lovely old house with no difficulty. Polly was in the garden in the company of their two dogs. She was busily scrubbing about in the border, clad in old clothes and wellies. The smile on her face as she caught sight of Melanie was a relief. She rubbed at her face, leaving a smudge on her cheek. 'Come on in,' she said. 'I've just had Linda on the phone. I've heard all about it. Or at least her side of it.' She kicked off her wellies in the porch. 'It's time I heard your version. Until then, I'm keeping an open mind.'

Melanie followed her through a cluttered hall into a cluttered sitting-room. Books were piled everywhere. Magazines littered the table. Sewing and knitting occupied most of the seats. 'Find a seat if you can,' Polly said easily. 'I would apologize for the mess. I feel I ought to but I never do. It's always like this. George and I are not tidy people. We used to blame the children, but now they're gone . . . ' She smiled, shooing the dogs off the sofa as they piled muddily onto it. 'I'll go and make some coffee. You're lucky. I've just made this sticky cake. Very bad for us. George eats all the things he tells other people not to.' She disappeared, the dogs going with her, and Melanie was left alone.

So far so good. Polly was willing at least to listen to her. She glanced curiously round the room. It was totally unexpected. The house exterior was rather grand, not preparing you for the happy-go-lucky state of the interior. There were a lot of family photographs, propped against dusty plants. Polly's plants needed a good talking to, Melanie reflected with a small smile. A heap of doggy toys and two battered bean-bags occupied most of what was a beautiful oriental rug. One of the dogs settled himself elaborately on the most battered bean-bag when Polly returned with the coffee. The other came over to Melanie and sniffed her legs appreciatively.

'Leave her, Sam.' Polly moved a pile of baby-blue knitting and sat down opposite Melanie. 'You don't mind dogs, do you?' she added. 'I can always shut them in the kitchen.'

'No, don't do that. I love them.' Melanie stroked the golden furry head that had been laid adoringly on her lap. 'Where shall I start, Polly?'

'Tell me about this man of yours.

Paul, is it? According to Linda, he barged in and told her he was a reporter. It transpires that you and he schemed to get this exclusive story, even going to the extraordinary lengths of you getting a job there.' She shrugged. 'That's about the gist of it. Except that Linda was obviously taken with Paul. She still swallows the charm like an innocent little girl.'

'Paul's not my fiancé any more,' Melanie began. 'And that's really all there is to it. He's determined to cause as much trouble for me as possible. I know I'm not blameless . . . I haven't been entirely honest with Linda.' She paused, the gentle warmth of the lovely creature beside her soothing her. 'I should have told her the truth. The engagement was ended when I went back home after the interview, but I pretended that all was well. It seemed simpler at the time,' she added with a rueful smile.

'Oh dear! Mention the press to Linda and she's like a tiger.' Polly clicked her tongue. 'She's brought it on herself. They've sensed a secret. It's what has kept the whole thing going. Philip never really suffered, not in the business sense, he was far too astute. Linda bore the brunt of it. They liked her face. Or disliked it. I don't know which. At any rate, it got so bad that at one time she hardly dare shake hands with another man in case someone snapped her and accused her of having an affair. They never forgave her Eleanor, you see. They wanted the marriage to fail. They certainly did their best to make it fail.'

'But Philip never believed any of it,' Melanie said thoughtfully. 'Their relationship must have been very strong.'

'He loved her. And she loved him. Desperately. That was why . . . ' Polly paused, looking carefully at Melanie as if assessing her for the first time. 'When Philip and Linda first met, Linda was so frightened that she might lose him. Philip seemed to take everything in his stride. Her extreme youth. Her bubbly looks. When he fell in love with her, he believed her to be not only a young but also an innocent girl. That meant a lot to him. He defended her reputation stoutly. That was why, of course, she could never bring herself to tell him.'

There was a moment's diversion as the two dogs solemnly changed places and Melanie's shoes were this time systematically sniffed. Melanie waited a little impatiently, sensing that Polly was about to break a confidence and tell her something very important.

'However, she was not innocent, not in the sense Philip thought. She had had a baby. A little boy. David. She was far too young. A stupid single night and that was it. Poor Linda!' She shook her head sadly. 'Medically there were complications and as a result she could not have any more children. Philip desperately wanted a son. She was terrified her gynaecologist would give the game away but he never did.'

'What happened to the baby? Was he adopted?' Melanie asked, trying to take in the implications of all this. To be married all those years and to keep a secret like that. It was incredible.

'She had an aunt. Her parents were dead by then, killed in a plane crash, but the aunt rallied round. She took care of the child on one condition. She did not want Linda to have any further contact with him. She meant it for the best . . . ' she added with a little smile. 'She took him with her to Canada and he was brought up there.'

'Did Linda ever see him?'

Polly nodded. 'One visit. She couldn't bear it. She had to see him. I believe the aunt had relented by then and they decided to tell him the truth. He'd always known the aunt was not his mother but it was still a surprise.'

'What a complicated life she's led,' Melanie said thoughtfully. 'I still can't quite believe that she managed to keep it a secret all those years.'

'Having an illegitimate baby mattered a great deal more in those days,' Polly said. 'She had already been branded as some sort of unsavoury girl and if they had found out about that, it would have really put the seal on it.' She smiled. 'More coffee? This is so difficult to talk about. I'm telling you, Melanie, so that you can understand her a little better. No wonder, is it, that she's so neurotic about the press? She dreaded them finding out and somehow blackmailing her. She said it would ruin all their lives and David was just starting out on his career.' She passed Melanie her coffee and a piece of cake. 'Don't dribble, Billy,' she said as he took up his begging position in front of Melanie.

'Where was I?' There was a twinkle in her eye as she regarded Melanie solemnly. 'You haven't guessed, have you? I thought you might when I mentioned Canada. David started out in Canada, you see, before moving to London. He's very talented, but then Linda's probably already told you that.'

'Christofer-Jon?' Melanie looked towards Polly for her acknowledgment of this remarkable fact. It pleased her. That explained everything. The secret meetings. The reason why Linda had to be discreet. 'Conrad saw them together once and jumped to the wrong conclusion.' She smiled. 'I'm glad he was wrong. I felt sure Linda wouldn't be having an affair with him. It didn't ring true to me.'

'Conrad . . . you mention Conrad . . . ' Polly's smile was wide. 'I'm sorry, it's really none of my business, but if you want to talk about it, please do. I believe he's going to America in a few days. Are you going to let him go?'

Melanie gave the last crumb of her cake to Billy and sighed. 'What can I do, Polly? He blames me for Helen breaking off their engagement. I've told him I had nothing to do with it but he's so . . . pig-headed,' she finished with feeling. 'He's so pig-headed that he's going to end up thousands of miles away from me. I just can't get through to him.'

'I'm so sorry.' Polly's voice was full of concern, her smile gone. 'If there's anything at all I can do to help, just ask.

And you must stay here for as long as you like. You can have one of the children's rooms. It'll be a bit untidy but you can help me get it shipshape later. Will you stay?'

'Thank you,' said Melanie simply. 'I don't know what I would have done if you'd turned me away.'

Polly shushed her, a little embarrassed. 'That'll be George,' she said thankfully as the dogs leapt towards the door, barking. 'Leave him to me, and leave Linda to me too. I'll go and see her and see if I can talk some sense into her. Apart from anything else, she needs you to help her finish this book.'

Left alone once more, Melanie moved towards the window. The sky was turbulent, a whirling wind whipping fine clouds across it. Soon Conrad would be up there, winging his way across the ocean. He might never come back. He would probably meet someone else and that would be that. He would remember her for a while but the memory would fade.

The door opened and George poked his head round it. 'Melanie! How nice to see you. I hear you're staying with us for a few days. Jolly good news.' He was shuffling from one foot to the other. He was an awkward man, Melanie realized, with affection, giving the impression that he was not very confident. But he was a doctor. Odd that! She imagined him listening sympathetically to his patients' problems. He was a good listener. 'The dogs are waiting,' he said. 'Are you ready?'

'What . . . ?' A little confused, Melanie followed him into the hall. The dogs had been told to sit. They had their leads on and a look of expectation on their faces.

'You take Sam.' He handed her the lead with the golden dog attached. 'I'll take Billy, he pulls a bit.'

They set off through the quiet village street, climbed over a stile, and let the dogs bound off once they were out of sight and sound of the road. The footpath dipped and there was sudden silence, broken only by the panting of the dogs as they searched frantically for new, exciting smells.

'Don't you worry about all this,' George said kindly. 'Polly will sort it out. She'll stand no nonsense from Linda. As for Conrad.' He gave her a quick sideways glance. 'He's finally decided to take up that offer, has he? I wish him well. It takes a brave man to tear up his roots and start something fresh.'

'I don't think he's quite sure where his roots are,' Melanie said reflectively. 'Half here and half there, I suppose.'

'And he's being pulled both ways.' George nodded. 'Difficult, eh? Sure you can't persuade him to stay.' His grin was crooked. 'A pretty girl like you?'

'I've tried, George. It's no use.' She clambered up the path as it took a sudden change of direction. George whistled for the dogs who were out of sight. 'Thanks for letting me stay,' she said. 'I could have gone home but . . . '

'I know. My children don't like

coming home either if something's not worked out. Parents understand more than you think sometimes.' He smiled a little. 'I take it you've still got something to prove to yourself.'

'For a start I can't leave Linda when she thinks so badly of me.'

'You shouldn't have let this ex-fiancé of yours get anywhere near her,' George pointed out sensibly. 'You know what she's like with men. She tends to believe everything they say.' He smiled broadly. 'And that's really not wise, is it?'

'Paul is very plausible. I'm not surprised she was taken in by him,' Melanie said with a worried attempt at a smile.

'Smoothie, eh?' They were nearly back at the road. George clipped the dogs' leads on before they reached the stile.

8

'What can I say? Will you ever forgive
me?' Linda gave her a quick hug. She
was wearing a coffee-coloured suit and
her manner was toned down to match.
'Polly was right, of course, I should
have allowed you to tell me everything.
The trouble was that man of yours was
so convincing. Sincere. Apologetic. He
was only telling me, he said, because his
conscience was troubled. He thought I
ought to be warned about you.' She
laughed shortly. 'In the end, I even
offered him an interview, would you
believe?'

Melanie shook her head, still amazed
by Paul. 'What else did he say?'

'That you and he had cooked it up
between you. You were to gain my
confidence, which you did, find out any
juicy bits, which you have, and report to
him. He was to zoom in for the

exclusive. He was working on something on the lines of 'The Fletcher-Grants — why no heir?' '

'Oh, no! Do you mean he'd found out about . . . ' Melanie hesitated briefly. 'About your son?'

Linda nodded. 'I'm glad you know. So silly, keeping it quiet all those years. Only Polly knew. But, suddenly, it doesn't matter any more. Looking back, I wonder if it would ever have mattered. Not to Philip. He loved me and he would have understood. He had become resigned to not having a son. As for David, well . . . he's so immensely talented . . . ' her eyes twinkled with pride and Melanie smiled for her, 'that it will make no difference to his career.'

She looked suddenly forlorn. Old. Melanie's sympathy welled up for her.

'I wouldn't blame you if you walked out on me after what I said,' Linda continued with a brave attempt at a smile. 'I'm not even sure I can do this book any longer. If I do, it will have to be the whole truth, including David.'

'I'm staying,' Melanie said firmly. 'You're not getting rid of me as easily as that. And we *are* going to finish this book. What is the deadline you keep mentioning?'

'Deadline?' Linda asked innocently. 'I really have no idea.' She glanced up as the clock chimed. 'If we start now, we can get two hours' work in before coffee . . . well . . . one hour at least. And tomorrow we'll start promptly. A very early start. Let's see . . . nine-ish? Or thereabouts,' she finished vaguely.

A sigh escaped Melanie. Linda needed to be chained down to her desk. She began to wonder seriously if this book would ever be written. Returning to her room, she unpacked again. Next time she packed, she vowed, it would be through her own choice. She did not want or expect a repetition of the last few traumatic days. She wanted to forget that. Quickly.

The phone rang and she picked it up idly, half expecting it to be Polly to enquire how she had got on.

'Sweetheart?'

'Conrad . . . ' she gasped. 'Oh, how wonderful to hear your voice.'

'It's lovely to hear you too. I had to ring . . . ' He was talking and she was trying to listen, but it was difficult to concentrate because she was so delighted by the unexpected call.

'I need to think for a while,' he was saying. 'You will try to understand, won't you?'

'I'll try . . . oh, Conrad, must you go? If you'd only asked me, I would have come with you.' There, it was said! There was no point at this stage in playing coy games with him. He knew how she felt about him. And she had spoken the truth. Her place was with him, wherever that happened to be. She twisted the cord of the phone anxiously. 'Where are you?'

'At the airport.' He laughed down the line. 'I've picked the wrong time to travel. I'm booked on a flight to Boston. When I get there, I'll stay overnight and

213

then drive up to Vermont to meet up with Bob at the site.'

'Has Bob got far to drive?' she asked. To be honest, she couldn't care less about how far Bob had to drive. She had just said the first thing that came into her head. Anything to keep him on the line. Her mind was blurring. There was so much she wanted to say, important things, and so little time to say them.

'He lives in Albany, New York State.' His voice was excited as he talked about places he knew. Somewhat sadly, Melanie listened as he briefly described the journey Bob would have to make.

'It sounds very nice,' she said, foolishly polite, when he had finished. Pips were going, perhaps he had no more change on him. 'I love you,' she blurted out, desperate that he should hear that.

'And I love you, Melanie.' His voice had softened, deepened, and she could see his face clearly as he said it. 'But I thought I loved Helen, you see.'

'But . . .'

'I've got to go. I've got to check in. Goodbye.'

Her reply strangled in her throat, but it was already too late. The line was dead.

* * *

'Would you mind, Linda, if I went up to the cottage and had a look round?'

'Not at all. I have a key somewhere.' She rummaged in her desk, producing a key and letting it hang loosely in her hand. She frowned slightly. 'Is it wise, Melanie? Might I offer a word of advice? Let him go, my dear. I know it's hard, but I think you have to face up to things. He's gone and he's going to busy himself in this project of his. What good is it going to do you going to the cottage? It's just going to bring everything back, isn't it?'

'I have to go,' Melanie said quietly. 'I know it'll be painful but it seems like the only way of . . .' She stopped. She wanted to say that she would be ridding her heart of him, but she found it impossible to say even to someone as sympathetic as Linda.

With a sigh, Linda passed her the key. 'It's pretty much as it was. He's just taken his personal things. Will you be all right going on your own?'

'Of course.' Melanie gave her a reassuring smile. She was not feeling suicidal, just extremely sad. She walked across the lawns down to the river, retracing their steps. The cottage looked sad too. She stared misty-eyed at it. She picked out a few weeds on her way to the front door. A cottage garden would have been so lovely. Scented. Softly-coloured flowers.

She opened the door. Silence. Already a faint mustiness and it had only been empty a short time. She peeped into the living-room. It looked exactly as it had before except for the missing photographs. He had taken Helen's photograph. She realized with a start that he had no photograph of her.

216

She had never thought to give him one. And he had never asked for one.

That would make it easier for him to forget her. With no picture of her to remind him, it would not be long before her memory became hazy. She wandered upstairs feeling just a little intrusive. The bedroom, the one he had used, was stark, impersonal, with a beamed ceiling and tiny window. Had he lain on this bed and thought about her? Had he woken up and thought about her?

She was going to cry. A sob escaped her as she went downstairs and into the kitchen. He had tried to tidy up. She gave a little smile as she noted his efforts. Everything had been pushed into one cupboard and was in great danger of falling out. Half crying, half smiling, she looked round. He had not emptied the bin and there was a letter in it. A letter torn into two pieces. She picked it out and pieced it together. Her name was written on the envelope.

She smoothed the paper and sat

down to read it. 'My darling Melanie,' he had written, 'I've been less than honest with you and it's time you knew the truth. About Helen. We knew each other a long time before it developed into something more than friendship. She's a solitary sort of person and it takes a long time to get to know someone like that. But, as time went on, it dawned on me that we were drifting apart. Hard as it was, I saw that I would have to break off the engagement. It was the right thing to do, to be fair to both of us. I kept putting it off. It never seemed the right moment. On the day of the accident, I finally told her. At first she was calm. She asked who I had met and when I told her there was nobody else, she laughed and said that we would work it out. It was just a temporary difficulty. I hated myself for what I was doing to her but part of me seemed to be looking on as if she was a stranger. We were at the cottage and suddenly she stormed out, grabbing the car keys as she went. Before I could stop her, she was in the car, in the driving-seat, about to drive off on her own. I managed to get into the passenger seat before she set off. She was furious and handling the car like a racing driver, a racing driver with four-inch heels. I tried to wrestle with her, tried to get her to stop before we reached the end of the lane and met up with traffic, but it was no use. The rest of what I told you was true. When they got her to hospital, she regained consciousness and, as they were preparing her for theatre, she looked at me and said 'You will stay with me now, won't you, Conrad?' It was the strangest feeling. As if she had deliberately crashed the car so that she could keep a hold on me. That's not true of course. How could it be? . . . Oh, Melanie, do you see what I'm trying to say?'

Melanie did see. *Now*. No, she couldn't believe it of Helen either. She would not have deliberately crashed the car so that she could have a hold on him. It had just happened and, afterwards, she had needed him. And being the man he was, he had stayed with her. He would have gone through with the marriage just as some sort of favour to her. With a sigh, Melanie returned her eyes to the letter and finished reading it. 'I owed it to her didn't I, Melanie? But then I met you. And I fell in love with you and I didn't know what to do any longer. And I still don't. That's why I'm writing to you to try and make it a little easier for you to understand. I know she's broken off the engagement but I still feel bound to her . . . '

It ended there. Unfinished. Thoughtfully, Melanie placed the letter in her pocket. Bound by a silken thread, she thought. She had never met Helen. She had no wish to meet Helen. But she saw her for what she was. As vindictive in her way as Paul had been in his. Using her illness to keep a firm grip on Conrad.

He had never sent her the letter. And

yet . . . had he meant her to find it? Why, oh why, hadn't he told her before? She could have helped him. Could have erased some of the guilt he felt. The tears were building up into a great tide of despair. She dropped her head onto her hands and wept.

★ ★ ★

Mindful of her mood next day but not asking questions, Linda was brisk and cheerful and they uncharacteristically got through a mountain of work.

It was during lunch that Linda casually broached the subject of Conrad. 'Feeling better, my dear?' she asked with a smile. 'I have to say this but, hurtful as it will be to you, it will pass, it will get easier. I felt exactly the same way when I met Philip and thought I was going to lose him. I didn't believe for one moment that he would have the courage to leave his wife for me.'

'But he did and it all turned out

happily for you,' Melanie said with a sad smile. 'At least . . . '

'I know what you mean.' Linda's eyes were bright. 'We had good times together. I have lovely memories. And so have you if you think about it. Hang on to those. No-one can take those away from you.'

'I feel . . . empty,' Melanie confessed. 'I'm trying. I know it's not the end of the world. I will forget him. In time. I may even meet someone else. But just now . . . it's very hard to bear.'

'He's a fool,' Linda said suddenly, changing tack. 'I can't understand him. He loves you. What's the matter with him? What's he gone to America for and left you here if he loves you? It was over between him and Helen long since, but neither of them would admit it.' She clicked her tongue crossly. 'He really is the most impossible man, and if he gets in touch with me I shall tell him exactly what I think of him.'

Melanie smiled her thanks. 'I told George that he was pig-headed and I'm right, aren't I? I even found myself wishing this business of his would fail,' she continued. 'But I couldn't be that mean. It means too much to him, so I hope it's a big success. Medieval banquets and serving-wenches included . . .' She finished with a little smile.

'Will they *really* go for that?' Linda frowned. She glanced at her watch. 'I'm exhausted. Do you think we've done enough for one day?'

'I thought we might start on your teenage years . . . ' Melanie said hopefully. 'It's going to be a bit delicate . . . '

'Delicate, my eye!' Linda said with a laugh. 'I shall tell the truth. I'm not ashamed of David . . . ' Her eyes twinkled. 'Even if he is a little naughty with the ladies. I really must get him to settle down, get married and give me some grandchildren.' Her eyes widened at the thought. 'Can you see me as a grandmother, my dear? What a role!'

'Shall we start on that now?' Melanie asked tentatively starting to arrange papers on her desk.

'Good heavens, no. I'm taking the afternoon off.' Linda flung her glasses aside. 'I've seen this beautiful evening dress. It's a most unusual blue, semi-fitted, about calf-length. I think I'll take a trip and buy it? Would you like to come with me?'

'No thank you.' Melanie replaced the top on her pen. Work over for another day!

With Linda gone, she spent the afternoon somewhat aimlessly, taking a walk in the grounds, enjoying the sunshine and trying to shake off the depression that was still wrapping itself round her. Back in her room, she glanced at the telephone. Conrad had promised to ring when he arrived. He would be there by now, in his beloved Vermont. He should be ringing any time now. She carried the phone over to the seat by the window so that she could look out onto the garden. She settled herself comfortably on the chair and kept the phone within easy reach.

'You can ring now,' she instructed it. 'I'm ready.'

It chose that precise moment to ring. She snatched eagerly at it, knowing that this time it was him. 'You've arrived,' she said, determined not to lose her composure. She had to start behaving like an adult woman, not some lovesick teenager.

'I've arrived,' he said. 'Were you waiting for me to call?'

'Yes.' She stared out of the window onto the lawns, the late sun streaking weakly across them. 'It's getting dark here,' she said. 'I can see the hills. They're beautiful, Conrad, edged in sunlight. The last of the sunlight. Just a pink glow.'

'Very poetical, my sweet.' He laughed. 'I can see hills too from where I am. They're every bit as beautiful as yours.'

'I wish I was with you.' She sighed down the line. 'You sound so clear. So near. I can hardly believe that you're thousands of miles away.'

He laughed and, miles away from him, she smiled. 'This call must be costing you a fortune,' she said. 'Can you afford it?'

'Just about. Aren't you going to ask me how the flight went?'

'If you insist. How did the flight go?'

'A bit bumpy. I was glad it was only three-quarters of an hour long.'

She stared blankly into the receiver. 'What are you talking about? It's over six hours, isn't it?'

'To Boston. Yes.'

'But that's where you are. Isn't it?'

'Whatever gave you that idea?' he asked innocently. His laugh this time was soft and husky, his voice penetrating and seductive. 'My love, I'm home. I'm on my way home to you. I'm looking at the same hills as you. The hills of home.' His voice caught with emotion.

She ignored the pretty words. 'What are you talking about?' she said crossly. 'You phoned me from the airport. You said you were about to

226

check in for your flight.'

'Perfectly true. Then I sat down and had a think. Helluva place to have a serious talk with yourself, but that's what I did. I wondered what the hell I was doing to contemplate leaving you, losing you. I cancelled the flight, spent the night in London and caught a shuttle up to Newcastle. I'm phoning from a pub on the way home. I've just stopped off for a quick bite.'

'Conrad Bailes!' Her mind was beginning to clear, a relief so great was beginning to overwhelm her. 'How dare you do this to me? How dare you let me think you were on the other side of the Atlantic? I thought I might never see you again.'

He laughed. 'Sorry about that. Did it upset you?' He ignored her explosion. 'I wrote you a letter but I never gave it to you. I'll tell you everything when I see you . . . '

'I know already,' she said quietly. 'It's all right, my love, I understand.'

'Would you like to move into the

cottage with me?' The question took her by surprise and she nodded into the phone, forgetting for a moment that he could not see her. 'After we're married of course,' he added hastily. 'Do you think anyone's listening in to this conversation because I want to tell you how much I love you and how desperate I am to get home to you.' There was a pause whilst she smiled and said nothing. 'I'm leaving now but I'll be with you very soon. Will you wait up for me?'

She found her voice. 'Conrad, let me get this straight,' she said. 'Have you just proposed? Because if so, I accept.'

'Oh good. I thought you might,' he said, so casually. 'You haven't answered the other part of the question and I'm getting funny looks at this end. It's not exactly private here.' He lowered his voice to a whisper. 'Will you wait up for me?'

Her voice was a low murmur. 'Of course I will.' She caught sight of her reflection. Happiness was spreading slowly through her. Through every vein. Pulsingly. Deliciously. The slow happy smile on her face was just the tip of it. She could not see Conrad but she knew he was smiling too.

THE END

CONFLICT OF HEARTS

Gillian Kaye

Somerset, at the end of World War I: Daniel Holley, unhappily married to an ailing wife and father of four grown-up children, is attracted to beautiful schoolteacher Harriet Bray, but he knows his love is hopeless. Daniel's only daughter, Amy, who dreams of becoming a milliner and is caught up in her love for young bank clerk John Tottle, looks on as the drama of Daniel and Harriet's fate and happiness gradually unfolds.

THE SOLDIER'S WOMAN

Freda M. Long

When Lieutenant Alain d'Albert was deserted by his girlfriend, a replacement was at hand in the shape of Christina Calvi, whose yearning for respectability through marriage did not quite coincide with her profession as a soldier's woman. Christina's obsessive love for Alain was not returned. The handsome hussar married an heiress and banished the soldier's woman from his life. But Christina was unswerving in the pursuit of her dream and Alain found his resistance weakening . . .